HOLLYWOOD VAMPIRE

A totally awesome collection of
ANGEL trivia

HOLLYWOOD VAMPIRE

A totally awesome collection of
ANGEL trivia

By
Keith Topping and Deborah Williams

First published in Great Britain in 2005 by
Virgin Books Ltd
Thames Wharf Studios
Rainville Road
London
W6 9HA

A catalogue record for this book is available from
the British Library.

ISBN 0 7535 1007 3

Typeset by Phoenix Photosetting, Chatham, Kent
Printed and bound in Great Britain by
Bookmarque Ltd

This book is *extremely* dedicated to

Kathy Sullivan [KT]

and

Rod Williams.
Just because. [DW]

CONTENTS

ACKNOWLEDGEMENTS

Keith Topping wishes to thank that old Scooby Gang of mine: Ian Abrahams, Kirstie Addis, Anna Bliss, Matt Broughton, Jason Boulter, Dave Cook, Scott Matthewman and all at *Buffy Watchers* (keep the faith), Suze Campagna, Martin Day, Clay and Kim Eichelberger, Robert Franks, Jeff Hart, Tony and Jane Kenealy, Shaun Lyon, Ian Mond, Mick Snowden, Graeme Topping, Jason Tucker, (the real) Maggie Walsh and Mark Wyman.

Deborah Williams would like to thank Amy Andrews, Betty Alyea, Moira Coxon, Rob Coxon, Lynn Delves, Penny Hodgkinson, Ann and Ted Hilton, Buddy Hollingsworth, Pat and John Laws, Jen McNabb, Deborah Mawaha, Janie Macintyre, Stephanie Newton, Christiana Raymond, Harold and Anne Raymond, Erica Reynolds, Sarah Ritchie, Sue Sharp, Jules Smith, Valerie West, Michelle Williams and Sharon Vernon.

'PREVIOUSLY ON *ANGEL*'

Born in Galway, in the eighteenth century, Liam was, according to Margaret, one of his subsequent victims, a drunken, whoring layabout and 'a terrible disappointment to your parents'. Though, as he would tell his vampire-sire Darla, with the exception of an honest day's work, there was virtually no challenge that he wasn't prepared to face.

After asking Darla to show him her world, Liam became a vampire in 1753. He has remained 27 years old ever since. Angel is the nickname of his possessing demon, *Angelus* ('the one with the angelic face'). He created havoc and blood-soaked carnage across Europe for decades and was, according to the elite vampire The Master, 'the most vicious creature I ever met'. Angelus's *modus operandi* involved sending his victims insane by killing their families and friends before, finally, murdering them.

However, all bad things come to an end and, in 1898 after he murdered a Romanian gypsy girl from the Kalderash Clan, Angelus was cursed by her people to regain his soul and have knowledge of the dreadful crimes he had committed.

Damned to walk the Earth, Angel – the vampire with a soul – spent most of the following century in abject misery over his past deeds, shunning other vampires, coming to America and, for a time, living in the gutter. Rescued by a friendly demon, Whistler, in New York in 1996 and shown a path of hope in the shape of the Slayer, Buffy Summers, Angel accepted that he had a destiny and travelled to Sunnydale and the Hellmouth.

Over the next three years Angel helped the Slayer and her friends – Willow, Xander, Cordelia, Giles and Oz – to fight the vampires, the demons and the forces of darkness. He killed his sire and nemesis, Darla, and assisted Buffy in her defeat of The Master and prevention of the opening of the Hellmouth.

Briefly, Angel lost his soul again after enjoying a moment of perfect happiness with Buffy. He returned to his evil ways, killing Giles's friend Jenny Calendar and stalking Buffy with the aid of his offspring, the English vampire couple Spike and Drusilla. Angel was eventually cured by a reversal spell performed by Willow and sent to Hell by Buffy to save the world from the coming of the demon Acathla.

On his return some months later, Angel slowly regained his humanity and resumed his relationship with Buffy. But he spent much time questioning the reason why he had been allowed to escape from Hell by The Powers That Be. Realising that there could be no future in a lasting relationship with Buffy, and after helping her defeat the apocalyptic schemes of Mayor Wilkins and the rogue Slayer Faith, Angel left Sunnydale for Los Angeles.

Settling in the City of Angels and trying to forget all about the girl he left behind, Angel spends his days brooding and his nights fighting evil and an ever-present craving for blood. Fortunately, he is contacted by half-human demon Francis Doyle, who points out the dangers of Angel's current lifestyle and informs him that The Powers That Be have chosen Angel for a special mission.

Guided by Doyle's visions, Angel tries to save the life of Tina, a coffee bar waitress who is being stalked by evil businessman and vampire Russell Winters. Sadly, Angel fails, but does succeed in killing Winters and saving Cordelia Chase, one of Buffy's Scooby Gang who has relocated to LA in the hope of becoming an actress.

Doyle, Cordy and Angel decide that they should start an agency and 'help the hopeless', and Angel Investigations is born ('City Of'). However, Angel has made a dangerous enemy in the evil law firm Wolfram & Hart and, specifically, lawyer Lindsey McDonald.

In a city singles bar, a demonic body-stealing entity is decimating the customers ('Lonely Heart'). Angel saves the day but seems in danger of losing his own heart to attractive detective Kate Lockley. Meanwhile, in Sunnydale, Spike has been searching for the famed Gem of Amara (a vampire Holy Grail which grants the undead invulnerability). Buffy obtains the gem and sends it to Angel via Oz. In an attempt to retrieve the gem, Spike kidnaps Angel and, with a psychopathic accomplice, subjects him to unbelievable torture ('In the Dark').

Angel Investigations next investigate a stalker who has the ability to detach parts of his own body and send them to prey on the object of his obsession ('I Fall To Pieces'). This case proves that, occasionally, the team *can* save the damsel *and* make some money. Distressed by her sub-standard apartment, Cordy is delighted when Doyle finds her new, plusher lodgings. The only snag is a resident ghost ('Rm W/a Vu').

The LAPD tries a sensitive approach to policing, with predictably chaotic results ('Sense and Sensitivity'). Doyle's former wife turns up wanting his blessing for her forthcoming wedding to a demon whose family want to eat his brains ('The Bachelor Party').

Doyle's attempts to pluck up the courage to ask Cordy on a date seem doomed to failure. Angel's love life is also in crisis as Buffy arrives in LA seeking a confrontation. An encounter with a Mohra demon restores Angel's humanity. After one perfect day of savouring the pleasures of the flesh Angel, unable to protect Buffy in his human form, asks the Oracles – The Powers' representatives – to fold back time. Angel is once again a vampire and only he retains his memory of the day he spent with Buffy ('I Will Remember You').

Doyle's visions lead the gang to a group of terrified demons that are hiding from The Scourge, an army of pure-bred demons intent on racial purification. Doyle, having confessed both his demonic nature and his love for Cordy, makes the ultimate sacrifice. He destroys The Scourge's death-ray at the price of his own life ('Hero').

A grieving Cordelia discovers that Doyle's parting kiss to her was more than a sweet goodbye to the object of his desire and she has to contend with painful visions and an empath demon named Barney, who wishes to sell her – newly acquired – gift of vision on the open market ('Parting Gifts'). Angel is assisted in saving her by rogue demon-hunter and former Watcher, Wesley Wyndam-Pryce. Wesley, another ex-Sunnydale resident, subsequently joins Angel Investigations.

Angel is tortured by dreams of his murderous past and is horrified when these dreams appear to be manifesting themselves in reality. The culprit, it turns out, is Penn, a serial-killing vampire sired by Angelus in his heyday. Angel tracks down Penn but in the process is forced to reveal his own vampiric nature to Kate Lockley ('Somnambulist').

Cordelia indulges in a one-night-stand and wakes up to find herself instantly and hugely pregnant. Thanks to Angel and Wesley, she is spawn-free within the day ('Expecting'). Angel encounters Jhiera, a militant feminist member of the Vigories – pan-dimensional female warriors who battle male oppression. Angel is sympathetic but cannot allow tourists to go around torching locals, however worthy their cause ('She').

Cordelia's visions enable the gang to save the life of a demonically possessed boy. An exorcism is arranged, but all is not as it seems. When Wesley confronts the released demon and taunts it with not getting the little boy's soul it replies 'What soul?' ('I've Got You Under My Skin').

Angel takes a flashback visit to his human past. He relives his awkward relationship with his father and his first days as Angelus while, in the present, trying and failing to save Kate's father – Trevor – from death at the hands of drug-dealing demons and their vampiric henchmen; a failure which further distances Angel from Kate ('The Prodigal').

Hired to investigate a kidnapping, Angel finds himself trapped in a demon fight club and forced to battle for his life and freedom while trying, with limited success, to incite his fellow prisoners to revolt ('The Ring'). Angel also meets another Wolfram & Hart nemesis, the alluring Lilah Morgan. Hollywood is a tough place for actors and soap-star Rebecca Lowell, upon discovering that Angel is a vampire, and being desperate to retain her own youth and beauty, feeds an unwitting Angel drugged wine thus, briefly, releasing Angelus ('Eternity').

The rogue Slayer Faith arrives in town direct from battling Buffy in Sunnydale and is recruited by Wolfram & Hart with a view to eliminating Angel ('Five by Five'). Capturing her former Watcher, Wesley, Faith subjects him to horrific torture as her real objective becomes clear. She wants to get Angel angry enough to kill her. Angel, however – despite the fierce opposition of Cordelia, Wesley and, especially, Buffy – decides to try rehabilitating her instead ('Sanctuary').

As Faith turns herself in and begins a prison sentence for her crimes, Angel encounters Charles Gunn, the leader of a street gang of itinerant vampire hunters. Gunn, while deciding that Angel poses no threat, is contemptuous of the idea of a good vampire, particularly one who is white and middle-class. Meanwhile, Cordy considers prostituting herself to millionaire computer geek David Nabbit whose path briefly crosses with that of Angel Investigations ('War Zone').

Angel encounters Wolfram & Hart's blind assassin, Vanessa Brewer, and infiltrates the firm, seeking the identity of Brewer's next target. In the process, and much to his surprise, Angel gains a new temporary ally – a conflicted Lindsey McDonald. However, Lindsey is subsequently lured back to the dark side by his boss, Holland Manners. Angel also acquires the mythical Scrolls of Aberjian ('Blind Date').

Wolfram & Hart, intent on destroying Angel's link to The Powers That Be, summon the demon Vocah in an attempt to regain the scrolls. Angel, with Wesley's help, learns the meaning of the Aberjian prophecy's key phrase, 'Shanshu': that the vampire with a soul will play an important part in the coming apocalypse and will then live until he dies. In other words, he will become human. Meanwhile, Wolfram & Hart recapture the scrolls to raise, from

Hell, the very thing that will tear Angel away from The Powers That Be, his sire Darla ('To Shanshu in LA').

Inspired by the prophecy, Angel starts to calculate his good deeds. However, his record suffers a setback when, due to mistaken identity, he kills the demon protector of a pregnant woman whose unborn child will have a significant future. Angel is compelled to become the woman's champion in a cross-dimensional trial of combat. Angel, Cordelia and Wesley also meet the Host – a green-skinned empath demon who runs a Downtown karaoke bar, Caritas. Meanwhile, Darla is recovering in the offices of Wolfram & Hart ('Judgment').

Wesley and Cordelia research the violent past of the abandoned Hyperion Hotel and are startled to learn that Angel was a resident there during the 1950s. Angel, attempting to help a young woman on the run from the police, was lynched by a paranoid mob of residents influenced by a Thesulac demon. Having abandoned both the hotel and its occupants to their fate, Angel is horrified to discover that the demon and his final victim are still in residence ('Are You Now or Have You Ever Been?').

Cordelia, Wesley and Angel also find the time to help Gunn's battle with the demon Deevak, after which Gunn becomes a member of the Angel Investigations team ('First Impressions'). Angel goes to the rescue of a lone girl in an alley menaced by thugs. But the girl, Bethany, aided by her telekinetic powers, is more than capable of looking after herself. The abused Bethany is actually being manipulated by Lilah Morgan for nefarious purposes ('Untouched').

Angel dreams of his first encounter with Drusilla and, unexpectedly, discovers that Darla is alive and has lured him into a trap.

Lindsey McDonald reveals that Wolfram & Hart's plan is not to kill Angel but to awaken his uglier urges in preparation for a forthcoming apocalypse ('Dear Boy'). Seeking spiritual guidance, Angel visits an upstate swami who isn't all that he seems. In Angel's absence, Wesley assumes the vampire's identity and, despite some bumbling along the way, manages to save the day *and* get the girl – a beautiful heiress, Virginia Bryce ('Guise Will Be Guise').

Angel continues to brood about Darla. This occurs as (the now human) Darla starts to feel the guilt and horror of her violent past. Lindsey, meanwhile, finds himself increasingly attracted to Darla and at odds with his superior's plans for her. When Wolfram & Hart decide to terminate their experiment, Lindsey gives this information to Angel, enabling the vampire to save his sire. A distraught Darla, tormented by her reacquired soul, begs her former lover to make her a vampire again. Angel, focused as ever on the possibility of redemption, refuses ('Darla').

Gunn's cousin becomes embroiled in an elaborate demon plot to steal the mythical Shroud of Rahmon – a cloth reputed to cause madness. Angel and Gunn infiltrate the gang but Wesley fears for Angel's sanity, especially after he – apparently – bites Kate Lockley during a confrontation ('The Shroud of Rahmon'). Darla's past, in the unwelcome shape of a syphilitic heart condition, finally catches up with her and Angel must choose between siring her again or watching her die. The Host, however, offers him another option – Angel can win a new life for Darla by submitting himself to three deadly trials. Sadly, there's a flaw in the plan and Angel, having endured excruciating torments, is told that Darla has already had her second chance. The pair decide to live out Darla's remaining days together but Wolfram & Hart have other ideas and bring Drusilla to LA, where she makes Darla a vampire again ('The Trial').

A desperate Angel searches for Darla's corpse, hoping to kill her before she can rise, but he's too late and Drusilla and Darla hit the streets on a murderous killing spree. An enraged Angel takes a terrible revenge on Wolfram & Hart, doing nothing to prevent Drusilla and Darla's massacre of the top echelon of the law firm, including Holland Manners. Returning to the Hyperion, he continues this flirtation with the dark side by firing Wesley, Cordelia and Gunn ('Reunion'). As his friends adjust to unemployment, Drusilla and Darla begin to recruit muscle for their own gang. But Angel gives the ladies a warmer welcome than they'd anticipated ('Redefinition').

Discovering that Wolfram & Hart are using a teen-shelter to siphon off monies raised for it, Angel visits the organiser, former Sunnydale resident Anne Steele. He then calls in a favour from fellow demon Boone to disrupt a charity function and expose the firm's criminal activities. Meanwhile, Cordelia, Wesley and Gunn decide to continue helping the helpless without their mentor ('Blood Money').

A brilliant scientist, Gene, heartbroken at hearing that his girlfriend plans to ditch him, decides to use his latest invention to trap himself and his lover forever in a single perfect moment of time. Unfortunately a demon sect alters his calculations, hoping to freeze the entire world. The Host and Angel prevent an apocalypse and comfort the hapless Gene while the Angel Investigations gang celebrate the successful conclusion of their first – solo – case ('Happy Anniversary').

The streets of LA seem to be getting safer, but it's not down to Angel or his friends. Rather, a squad of zombie policemen who are keen on justice, if not mercy, are terrorising Anne's street kids. Wesley helps Gunn to solve the problem but ends up in hospital with a near fatal gunshot wound. Kate's career is placed on the line after she tries to help Angel ('The Thin Dead Line'). Things aren't going well for Wesley, Cordelia and Gunn's new business after a client refuses to pay their bill.

Meanwhile, Wolfram & Hart are gearing up for the 75-year review and, facing the arrival of a Senior Partner, nervous lawyers seek help via evil rituals. It seems that a Wolfram & Hart contract extends well beyond death as Holland Manners takes Angel on a trip to the Home Office, revealing in the process that Los Angeles is (as many had believed all along) Hell. As Cordelia and Kate face (separate) mortal danger, Angel succumbs to the pleasures of Darla's bed and staggers into the rain in agony, just as he once did after having sex with Buffy ('Reprise').

However, this is an epiphany of perfect despair rather than happiness and Angel, much to Darla's disgust, emerges from his night of passion with his soul intact. Kate attempts suicide but Angel, with some supernatural help, saves her. Then, guided by the Host's warning that his friends are in danger, he attempts to rebuild some burned bridges. Lindsey, meanwhile, has a few scores of his own to settle with Angel.

Having saved Cordelia's life, Angel tells Wesley that he doesn't want his friends to return to work for him. Rather, he would like to work for them, having seemingly recovered his taste for their mission ('Epiphany').

Harmony Kendall drops in to visit her old friend Cordelia, but Harmony has changed since her Sunnydale days – she's now a vampire and part of a vampiric pyramid scheme. Meanwhile, Angel discovers that there's an even bigger bitch than Harmony – atonement ('Disharmony'). Lindsey's life was difficult with the prosthetic hand that he was forced to wear after Angel chopped off his own, but his newly acquired replacement proves to be a mixed blessing. Cordelia's latest horrifying vision leads the team to Wolfram & Hart's body-parts farm. Lindsey leaves Wolfram & Hart and Angel intervenes to save his nemesis's life – but he cannot resist one final bit of payback ('Dead End').

Cordelia's dreams of acting stardom are compromised by a lecherous director and Angel's protective attitude, while a disturbance at Caritas has the Host seeking Angel's help. The trail leads to a library, a missing student and a mysterious book in an unreadable language. The Host reveals that he is Lorne (Krevlornswath of the Deathwok Clan), a native of another dimension, Pylea. He finds himself face to face with a past that he would rather forget when Cordelia is sucked through a portal to his former home ('Belonging').

In Pylea, Cordy is treated as a slave and meets another LA resident, missing physicist Fred Burkle, who has been stuck there for five years. Back in LA, the gang frantically search for a way to rescue their colleague. Arriving in Pylea, Lorne mourns the presence of his far-from-loving family (although it's hard not to love his brother, the dancing Numfar), while Angel celebrates the fact that the suns in this world are both of the non-fatal variety. Cordelia's visions surprisingly elevate her status from slave to princess. Her would-be rescuers, on the other hand, are captured ('Over the Rainbow').

Cordelia quickly finds that she is nothing more than a figurehead monarch, but is happy to meet her handsome half-human champion, the Groosalugg. Pylea brings out the worst in Angel – quite literally ('Through the Looking Glass'). Angel, with Fred's help, battles his manifest demon while Wesley and Gunn become free-

11

dom fighters in a revolutionary cause. Lorne loses his head, which luckily proves not to be fatal. Having set Pylea on the road to freedom and independence, the gang help Fred to reopen the portal and return to LA. There, Willow waits for them with the terrible news of Buffy's death ('There's No Place Like Plrtz Glrb').

Fred has difficulties adjusting to life back in her own dimension as Angel returns from a summer in Sri Lanka, where his attempts to come to terms with Buffy's demise have been hampered by the attentions of some demon monks. His first mission back in LA involves liquidating a group of vampires whose number include Elizabeth, the eternal love of James – one of Angelus's protégés during the 1760s. Heartbroken at Elizabeth's death and swearing revenge, James visits a demon doctor who renders him temporarily invincible. Angel ultimately defeats James, but is left to question his own response to the death of his true love. Meanwhile, in Nicaragua, a heavily pregnant Darla seeks some answers of her own ('Heartthrob').

Cordelia's visions begin manifesting themselves in a physical way. However, as the gang seek a mystical cure, Lorne reveals that the visions are being sent not by The Powers but, rather, by Wolfram & Hart, who need Angel to open a door between dimensions and spring one of their clients from Hell. Angel overcomes Skip, a demonic prison guard, rescues his charge and ensures that Lilah Morgan will never again attempt to use Cordelia as a pawn ('That Vision Thing').

An outbreak of seemingly random killings of the LA demon community leads Gunn to his old gang, and a hard decision as to where his loyalties lie. Cordelia seeks the help of the Transuding Furies (who seem *very* well acquainted with Angel) to temporarily lift the protective Sanctorium spell on Caritas and enable him to rescue his friends from a lengthy stand-off. Gunn decides that his old gang have lost the mission and that his allegiance is with Angel ('That Old Gang of Mine').

Investigating a series of bizarre deaths, Angel visits a health club and, later, a retirement home. There, he encounters Marcus, an elderly man who has, literally, recaptured his youth by taking over the bodies of healthy young men. In Angel, Marcus finally finds a body that may be strong enough to withstand this process for longer than a single night. Angel finds himself trapped in the body of a weak-hearted old man until his friends realise what has happened and reverse the spell ('Carpe Noctem'). Fred is visited by her parents and must finally face up to what happened to her in Pylea. While largely supportive of her new lifestyle and friends, the Burkles offer Fred the sanctuary of a return home. However, she chooses to stay at the Hyperion, where her intellect and inventiveness are proving increasingly helpful in the fight against evil ('Fredless').

Billy Blim, the demonic captive whom Angel rescued from hellfire, wastes no time in unleashing the primal rage inherent in any male he touches; his victims fall prey to murderous misogynistic urges. Wesley, Gunn and Angel are no exception and Fred and Cordelia must fight for their lives until Lilah, having been savagely beaten by her colleague Gavin Park, sends Billy back to Hell. Wesley, devastated by his actions towards Fred, struggles to regain his sense of self despite Fred's assurances that he is a good man ('Billy').

As a hugely pregnant Darla arrives at the hotel, Angel is forced to contemplate the seemingly impossible consequences of his night of passion with her some months ago. His friends also discover that the child of two vampires is the subject of yet another ancient prophecy. Meanwhile Sahjhan, a non-corporeal demon, concerned that Angel's yet-to-be-born child is a threat to his life, releases Angel's old enemy, the vampire hunter Daniel Holtz, from a stone sarcophagus in which he was been encased for two centuries ('Offspring').

Wolfram & Hart are intent on capturing Darla for their own nefarious purposes and Angel must protect her from both the law firm and a sinister vampire cult that believes that their baby is the Miracle Child. Holtz catches up on the events of the past 227 years and plans revenge for Angelus and Darla's heartless murder of his family ('Quickening').

Darla, influenced by the soul of her unborn child, experiences love for the first time, but Holtz is on the trail and attacks Caritas, forcing the gang to flee to an alley where Darla, unable to give birth, makes the ultimate sacrifice, staking herself to save her child's life. Thus, she leaves Angel to face fatherhood and the possible consequences of the prophecy alone ('Lullaby'). As Angel seeks to protect his newborn son, Connor, from the assaults of the demon underworld and the machinations of Wolfram & Hart, Holtz recruits a troop of individuals who have lost their family to vampires, including the beautiful and dangerous Justine Cooper. Under siege from his enemies, Angel flees the Hyperion and lures the warring factions into an explosive trap in the desert ('Dad').

On her birthday, Cordelia experiences a vision so intense that she leaves her body. As her friends struggle to bring her back from the astral plane, Cordy takes a trip with the demon Skip, who tells her that she was never meant to have the visions and offers her a chance to change her life. In the ensuing alternate reality, Cordelia has become a successful sitcom actress haunted by the vague feeling that her destiny remains elsewhere. When she meets this universe's shattered version of the Angel Investigations team, she asks Skip for her old life back. Since, as a human, the visions will ultimately prove fatal, Skip demonises Cordelia, giving her pain-free visions and, as a bonus, the gift of levitation ('Birthday').

Angel becomes obsessed with the need to provide for his family and advertises for clients, thus unwittingly leading his team into danger from a group of demons who want Fred's head for their dying leader ('Provider'). An evening at the ballet takes a sinister turn as Angel spots something odd about this particular production – it seems to have remained remarkably unchanged for over a century. Angel and Cordelia go backstage to investigate and are possessed by the spirits of unrequited lovers. Meanwhile, Wesley plucks up the courage to profess his love to Fred, unaware that Gunn has similar ideas ('Waiting in the Wings').

Fred and Gunn embark on a romantic relationship just as Angel finds his relationship with Cordelia altered by the arrival from Pylea of the handsome Groosalugg. Not only is Angel forced to confront his own shortcomings as a champion but he also agrees to help Cordelia find a magical prophylactic that will enable her to consummate her passion for Groo without losing her visions ('Couplet').

Wesley investigates a prophecy which suggests that Angel will eventually kill Connor. To his distress, the signs of the prophecy's fulfilment all seem to be coming true ('Loyalty'). Angel, unaware that his food has been spiked by Wolfram & Hart with his son's blood, is behaving in an erratic fashion, terrifying Wesley, who kidnaps Connor in an attempt to keep the baby safe. Sadly, he plays into the hands of Holtz and Justine and is left for dead with his throat cut as Holtz takes Connor through a dimensional portal to Quor-Toth, darkest of the dark dimensions ('Sleep Tight').

A grief-stricken Angel seeks revenge on Wesley, attempting to suffocate him in his hospital bed. Wesley finds himself ostracised by his friends as Fred, Gunn and Angel pay a visit to the chaos-loving guardian of Wolfram & Hart's White Room. Angel conjures dark magic in an attempt to rescue his son from the Hell dimension. But the portal to Quor-Toth can only be opened once; a second attempt would endanger the universe ('Forgiving'). A depressed Wesley learns from Fred that the prophecy for which he almost gave his life was a fake and his efforts were for nothing. A supernatural repo-man has come to collect a debt from Gunn – his soul, signed away in return for a truck. Angel is forced to put his own soul on the line to save that of his friend ('Double or Nothing').

As a result of Angel's use of dark magic, the Hyperion is infested with supernatural parasites that inhabit and dehydrate their victims. Fred is infected and her friends must turn to Wesley for help. Meanwhile, Cordelia discovers that she possesses new and shocking powers and the team learn of the coming of The Destroyer as an unexpected guest arrives at the hotel ('The Price').

Connor returns from Quor-Toth as a feral teenage warrior who has been taught to hate his biological father and to seek vengeance for the deeds of Angelus. When his attempt to kill Angel fails, Connor must learn to adapt to life alone in a bewildering and terrifying city ('A New World'). Angel and Connor reunite and fight side by side, but Holtz has a final devious plan, staging his own death at the hands of Justine and framing Angel for the deed ('Benediction').

As Lilah and Wesley enter into a sexual alliance, Connor, enraged by Holtz's death, plans revenge on his father. Unaware of this, Angel and Cordelia arrange to meet and discuss their relationship but en route Cordelia is sent a message from The Powers That Be and, escorted by Skip, ascends to her destiny as a Higher Being. Connor ambushes Angel and, assisted by Justine, locks him in a steel coffin and sinks him to the bottom of the ocean ('Tomorrow').

With Angel starving and hallucinating on the ocean floor and Cordelia bored on a different plane of existence, Fred and Gunn search for clues as to where their friends have disappeared to. However, salvation for Angel comes from an unlikely source as Wesley holds Justine hostage to aid in a search and rescue operation. Meanwhile, Connor finds his double dealing exposed and is brought face to face with his father who, after telling him that he loves him, kicks him out of the Hyperion to fend for himself ('Deep Down').

The search for Cordelia continues and, guided by Wesley, Angel visits Dinza, a Dark Goddess of the lost, who tells Angel about the Axis of Pythia, a mystical antiquity that can locate souls. Angel, Gunn and Fred break into an auction house to recover the artefact, only to discover that Gwen Raiden, a glamorous cat burglar with electrical superpowers, has beaten them to it ('Ground State'). In need of a break, Angel and his friends head for Las Vegas to visit Lorne, who has become a huge cabaret celebrity. But all is not well with the empath demon as he is being forced to read the minds of his audiences and help crooked casino owner Lee Demarco steal their destinies ('The House Always Wins').

An amnesic Cordelia returns to this plane of existence. Angel decides to protect her from the full reality of her past. But Lorne's attempt to read Cordelia and thus help her to regain her memories backfires when Wolfram & Hart brain-suck him, stealing what he saw in Cordelia's mind ('Slouching Towards Bethlehem').

Fred has a physics article published and is invited to speak at a high-profile symposium. During her speech a dimensional portal opens and she narrowly escapes being drawn into it. Research shows that Fred's old professor has been banishing his brightest students to other dimensions, including Fred herself to Pylea. Enraged, Fred plots a suitable revenge but Gunn prevents her from committing murder at a terrible cost to their relationship. Meanwhile, Cordelia bonds with Connor and slowly pieces together some aspects of her past life ('Supersymmetry').

Lorne casts a spell to restore Cordelia's memory with disastrous effects as all of the Angel Investigations team regress to their teenage personas. Once the spell is broken, however, Cordelia's memory returns ('Spin the Bottle').

As Angel and his friends struggle to deal with a sudden spate of biblical plagues, Cordelia has a vision that is beyond her worst nightmares. With Lilah's reluctant help, Angel, Wesley, Gunn and Lorne investigate and meet a formidable new enemy, The Beast. As fire rains down on Los Angeles, Connor and Cordelia take their relationship to a disturbing new level, unaware that Angel is watching them ('Apocalypse Nowish').

The Beast kills its way through LA, trapping Connor inside Wolfram & Hart as Angel and his friends find their rescue mission complicated by hordes of zombie employees. At the Hyperion, Angel confronts Cordelia and instructs her to take her new boyfriend and get the hell out ('Habeas Corpses').

The Beast is systematically exterminating all five members of the Ra–Tet, an ancient mystical order. Once he accomplishes his goal, he will be able to blot out the sun, plunging LA into eternal darkness. Gwen helps the team by providing a refuge for Manjet, the last of the five. But even she is unable to prevent Manjet's murder. Learning from Cordelia that Angelus has a past history with The Beast, the team decide that it's time to call back Angel's own personal demon ('Long Day's Journey').

As LA stews in its own darkness, Wesley summons a mystic shaman to release Angelus. Angel experiences a fantasy of a perfect day. But, as he achieves perfect happiness in the arms of Cordelia, his soul is extracted and stored in a mystical vessel, and Angelus returns ('Awakening'). As Connor valiantly struggles to contain the crime wave that engulfs the city, Angelus uses mockery to sow the seeds of discord among the Angel Investigations team. Cordelia offers to sacrifice herself to Angelus in return for information. Intrigued, Angelus agrees ('Soulless').

The team discover that Angel's soul is missing and Cordelia has a vision telling her how to restore it; however, despite the apparent success of the ritual, Angelus is still very much in charge of Angel's body. He's also free from his prison, as Lilah discovers when she arrives at the Hyperion armed with a crowbar and intent on revenge. However, it is *not* Angelus who kills Lilah soon afterwards, but rather Cordelia who has, seemingly, planned Angelus's escape ('Calvary').

Believing that Angelus was responsible for Lilah's death, Wesley decapitates her corpse to prevent her from rising. Angelus enjoys his freedom and discovers that something other than The Beast is behind the apocalyptic events in LA. He also discovers, to his annoyance, that killing The Beast restores the sun to the city. Meanwhile, Wesley helps rogue Slayer Faith to stage a jailbreak in order to recapture Angelus. And Cordy tells Connor that she is expecting his child ('Salvage').

As Cordelia's pregnancy advances at unnatural speed, she begins to exhibit strange new powers. Faith tracks and fights Angelus, who is being guided by a strange inner voice, which he believes belongs to The Beast's master. But in biting and drinking from Faith, Angelus unwittingly finds himself drugged by her tainted blood ('Release'). Angelus takes a nightmare trip into his own past, accompanied by the Slayer. Fred seeks help from Sunnydale, contacting Willow to find and restore Angel's soul ('Orpheus').

While the team come to terms with the ramifications of Cordelia's pregnancy, and seek the identity of The Beast's master, Gwen asks for Gunn's help in freeing a kidnapped child. However, Gwen is not telling the whole truth and Gunn finds himself helping her steal a device that will enable Gwen to control her powers. Back at the Hyperion, Cordelia's perfidy is exposed ('Players').

Seeking answers about who, or what, is controlling Cordy, Angel pays a visit to Skip. However, the answers that he receives are profoundly disturbing and leave the team contemplating their lack of free will. Cordy, meanwhile, enlists Connor's help in obtaining the ingredients required for a protective ritual and, despite an attempted intervention by his ghostly mother, Darla, he assists in the murder of a young girl as Cordelia goes into supernatural labour. Angel tracks her down but is unable to kill her before her child is born. At which point, he and Connor fall to their knees in awe as Jasmine enters the world ('Inside Out').

The messianic Jasmine, a Power That Was, announces her intent to save the world from itself and she is welcomed with open arms by Angel and his friends, who become her devoted disciples. But, although Jasmine radiates peace and happiness, Fred sees her true face after coming into contact with her blood. As Jasmine gathers new converts, Fred is forced to flee ('Shiny Happy People'). Los

Angeles is rapidly becoming a utopian paradise, with Jasmine's eating of a few of her own acolytes going quietly unnoticed amid the atmosphere of peace, love and harmony. Fred researches mind control techniques and realises that blood is the key to stopping Jasmine. She devises a plan to enable the team to see the true face of their goddess. However, although she is mostly successful, the revelation fails to work on Connor ('The Magic Bullet').

Angel and his friends flee underground to escape the wrath of Jasmine's followers. Wesley learns that Jasmine is from another dimension and that the answer as to how to destroy her is discovering her true name. Angel and Wesley obtain a blue orb that enables Angel to open a portal to Jasmine's home dimension ('Sacrifice'). There, Angel climbs a mountain and battles with the keeper of the sacred word. He is victorious and, returning to our reality, the keeper speaks Jasmine's name, revealing her true face and causing panic and mayhem. Seeking vengeance, Jasmine intends to destroy humanity, but she is killed by Connor before she can carry this out ('Peace Out').

Jasmine's death puts an end to world peace and Angel and his friends face the consequences of their actions. The shattering of Connor's illusions leads him to become unstable, Cordelia remains in a coma and Lilah returns from the dead to make the team an unbelievable offer – to take over Wolfram & Hart. Each member is tempted, Wesley by unlimited access to books and texts, Fred by the scientific research department of her dreams and Lorne by the prospect of working with everyone he's ever wanted to meet, while Gunn has a life-changing encounter with a black panther in the White Room. Angel, ultimately, makes the decision on their behalf: offered the chance to bend time and give the tormented Connor a normal life, he signs on the dotted line and a new era begins for the Angel Investigations team ('Home').

21

Angel and his friends find themselves in charge of the LA offices of Wolfram & Hart, with many evil clients – and more than a few evil employees – to worry about. They are plunged into a race against time to prevent a threatened apocalypse. Gunn gets a brain upgrade which, combined with Angel's ultraviolence, saves the day. But at what cost? As Angel and his friends consider the consequences, a mysterious amulet disgorges an unhappy and not altogether welcome visitor ('Conviction').

As Angel and his friends adjust to Spike's ghostly presence, a necromancer – enraged that Angel's closure of the internment acquisitions department has cut his supply of corpses – attempts to conspire with Spike to destroy Angel's soul ('Just Rewards'). Angel's destruction of a werewolf comes too late to save Nina Ash from infection. Angel and his friends must find the new werewolf and teach her how to control the beast within. But an evil restaurateur is also tracking her ('Unleashed').

If Fred can defy most of the laws of physics, she believes that she can make Spike corporeal again. Spike, meanwhile, is suffering from terrifying hallucinations as the evil spirit Pavayne tries to drag him into Hell ('Hellbound'). Lorne, overwhelmed by the pressure of organising Wolfram & Hart's Halloween party, has his sleep removed. To hilarious and deadly effect ('Life of the Party'). A dramatic encounter with Wolfram & Hart's aged mail delivery guy sets in motion a bizarre chain of events that culminates in Angel fighting an ancient Aztec demon with the help of some undead Mexican wrestling brothers ('The Cautionary Tale of Numero Cinco').

Wesley, guilt stricken after Fred is wounded, is shaken by the arrival of his father. Roger Wyndam-Pryce wants his son to rejoin the ranks of a reformed Council of Watchers. Matters are further complicated when ninja cyborgs attack the building ('Lineage'). A power surge from a mysterious package recorporealises Spike, but his celebrations are interrupted by a wave of insanity among Wolfram & Hart's employees. The presence of two ensouled vampires may have thrown the universe out of balance. Angel and Spike must fight to drink from a magical cup to discover which of them the Shanshu prophecy applies to ('Destiny').

Harmony, now working as Angel's PA, has a really bad day, culminating in finding a dead man in her bed. Especially as Wolfram & Hart's zero-tolerance policy towards murder may result in the termination of more than her employment ('Harm's Way'). Angel also feels disconnected from his friends and his dreams take a decidedly odd turn. Meanwhile, Spike has found a new best friend – a man who calls himself Doyle and who alleges that he gets visions from The Powers That Be ('Soul Purpose').

A hyperstrong teenager escapes from an LA psychiatric ward and unleashes carnage. Angel and his friends realise that she is a Slayer. Meanwhile, an old acquaintance arrives to help out ('Damage'). Bitterly disillusioned with life, Angel threatens to resign. However, Cordelia emerges from her coma with a vision that leads Angel into battle against a vengeful Lindsey McDonald ('You're Welcome').

Angel's past comes back to haunt him in the form of a young submariner he encountered in 1943. His wartime exploits in a captured Nazi submarine now have potentially lethal consequences for his friends ('Why We Fight'). When several children are hospitalised, apparently due to the malign influence of the puppet TV show *Smile Time*, Angel investigates, then wishes that he hadn't when he's hexed and muppetised ('Smile Time').

When Fred opens a mysterious stone sarcophagus she becomes infected by a deadly pathogen. Spike and Angel rush to England to visit the Deeper Well and find a cure before Fred is consumed by Illyria, an Old One seeking to return to this dimension. But the price for Fred's life is too high for her friends to pay and Fred dies in the arms of a devastated Wesley ('A Hole in the World').

Angel reasons that death doesn't have to be the end. With this in mind, Fred's friends desperately seek a way to bring her back. However, Wesley realises that this is futile. Meanwhile, Knox's perfidy is revealed and Gunn finds that he was manipulated into helping with the conspiracy that ended with Fred's death ('Shells').

While a grieving Wesley helps Illyria to adapt to this dimension, Angel and Spike find Eve in hiding and seek answers about The Senior Partner's part in their ongoing troubles. With Gunn, they enter a Wolfram & Hart holding dimension to save Lindsey from a personal Hell. But, again, there is another huge price to be paid; in order to rescue Lindsey, a repentant Gunn must take his place ('Underneath').

Angel is shocked when his son Connor is brought into his office by his new parents, who are alarmed by their son's apparent superpowers. Initially reluctant to become involved, Angel relents when the family are attacked by demons. Angel trains Connor to fulfil the prophecy by killing Sahjhan to prevent the sorcerer Cyvus Vail from revealing his darkest secret. But, a suspicious Wesley discovers that his memories have been altered ('Origin').

Illyria rescues Gunn from the holding dimension but her powers are becoming unstable and her time-slipping abilities threaten Angel's friends and, indeed, LA itself. Aided by Angel's own time-travelling experiences, Wesley stabilises Illyria and, in doing so, limits her powers. Meanwhile, Eve's replacement as liaison to The Senior Partners, the mysterious Marcus Hamilton, arrives ('Time Bomb').

Angel and Spike's Italian job is to travel to Rome and bring back the head of a demon. And, as a side-issue, they also attempt to save their former lover, Buffy Summers, from the perceived sinister clutches of their arch-nemesis, the (allegedly) evil Immortal ('The Girl in Question').

Angel seems to be drifting towards the dark side and his questionable judgements are causing concern. However, once his friends are told of his daring plan to bring down the evil Circle of the Black Thorn, they back him, despite the certainty that doing so will unleash the full wrath of The Senior Partners ('Power Play').

Angel and his friends prepare for apocalypse by living one last day to the full then, facing insurmountable odds and in the knowledge that their survival is unlikely, they go to work and pass into legend ('Not Fade Away').

AWESOME!!!
The finest 25 episodes of *Angel*

Here is that imaginary desert island five-DVD box set of *Angel* episodes that is, quite simply, impossible to live without. Just imagine how empty and worthless your lives would be if – like Liam – you'd been born in the eighteenth century and, as a consequence, never got to see any of the following.

'Smile Time' (episode 102)
Demons try to steal the souls of children through a TV show and when Angel intervenes, he's turned into a puppet.

'A Hole in the World' (episode 103)
Infected by a deadly pathogen, Fred Burkle is dying. Her friends desperately search for a cure.

'Waiting in the Wings' (episode 57)
A night at the ballet turns decidedly supernatural, with some particularly erotic results for Angel and Cordelia.

'Through the Looking Glass' (episode 43)
In the fairytale dimension of Pylea, Cordy becomes royalty, Wes and Gunn start a revolution, Lorne loses his head and Angel is turned into a monster.

'Five by Five' (episode 18)
Wolfram & Hart employ the rogue Slayer Faith to assassinate Angel.

'Darla' (episode 29)
As Angel and his friends search for a now human Darla, Angel remembers the key events in their 250-year relationship.

'You're Welcome' (episode 100)
Cordelia Chase comes out of a coma with a mission – to save Angel from himself.

'The Girl in Question' (episode 108)
Angel and Spike travel to Italy, ostensibly to collect a dead demon's head but in reality to save Buffy Summers from her latest boyfriend.

'Not Fade Away' (episode 110)
Facing the final battle with the Circle of the Black Thorn, Angel and his friends have one final day to enjoy life before almost certain death.

'Birthday' (episode 55)
On Cordelia's birthday, a violent vision puts her on another astral plane, where she is informed that it was never her destiny to be who she is.

'The House Always Wins' (episode 69)
Following Lorne to Las Vegas, Angel, Gunn and Fred find themselves in the middle of a sinister scheme to steal the futures of hotel guests.

'Somnambulist' (episode 11)
Angel suffers from disturbing killing dreams that subsequently seem to be coming true. Can he really have reverted to his evil self?

'Disharmony' (episode 39)
Harmony Kendall comes to LA to look up her old Sunnydale mucker Cordelia. But no one has bothered to inform Cordy of a significant lifestyle change that her friend has gone through.

'Are You Now or Have You Ever Been?' (episode 24)
In 1952, Angel was living in the Hyperion Hotel in Hollywood and witnessed the rampant paranoia of the times, exacerbated by a Thesulac demon. Now, 50 years later, those events return to haunt him.

'Spin the Bottle' (episode 72)
An attempt by Lorne to provide a magic cure to Cordelia's amnesia has disastrous (if amusing) side effects as Cordy, Angel, Gunn, Fred and Wesley revert to their teenage personalities.

'Rm W/a Vu' (episode 5)
Doyle finds Cordelia a new apartment. Unfortunately, a couple of previous inhabitants haven't left there yet, despite their deaths.

'Billy' (episode 50)
A terrible violence erupts within Angel Investigations when a demonic young man, Billy Blim, releases primal rage in his male victims.

'Reunion' (episode 32)
Drusilla and a newly revampirised Darla go on a killing spree in LA with the upper echelons of Wolfram & Hart as their main target. Strangely, Angel doesn't seem to care.

'Orpheus' (episode 81)
Spiked by Faith's drug-tainted blood, Angelus spirals back into the private hell of the last century of Angel's past. Meanwhile, Fred seeks help in restoring Angel's soul, and finds it in Sunnydale.

'To Shanshu in LA' (episode 22)
Wolfram & Hart summon Vocah to retrieve the Scrolls of Aberjian from Angel. They are needed to raise the one thing that will tear Angel away from his link to The Powers That Be. Darla.

'Dead End' (episode 40)
Lindsey McDonald is given a transplant by Wolfram & Hart but to whom did the replacement evil hand originally belong and why is it constantly writing the word 'kill'?

'Guise Will Be Guise' (episode 28)
With Angel out of town, Wesley assumes his identity to take a case *and* save the girl.

'Loyalty' (episode 59)
Wesley's worst fears are confirmed – the prophecy that he has interpreted is true. 'The father will kill the son.'

'That Old Gang of Mine' (episode 47)
Someone is killing Los Angeles' demons and Gunn must choose sides when he discovers that his old street gang are responsible for the murders.

'Epiphany' (episode 38)
Lorne tells Angel that his friends are in danger and he determines to win back their loyalty. If he can get to them before they all die.

WELL, *THAT* SUCKS!!!

The five worst episodes of *Angel*

... And then, sadly, there is that handful of episodes that you would gladly bury on a desert island to avoid ever having to see again.

'She' (episode 13)
Angel becomes involved in a pan-dimensional battle between Jhiera, a female Vigorie, and her male oppressors. A heavy-handed piece full of rad-fem nonsense that also seems to be an abandoned *Deep Space Nine* script that somehow ended up in the *Angel* office by accident.

'I Fall to Pieces' (episode 4)
A woman hires Angel Investigations to protect her from her doctor, who is stalking her and can remove his own body parts to indulge in nefarious skulduggery. (Even the production team themselves weren't oblivious to this one's faults, making a joke of it in 'Through the Looking Glass'.)

'The Cautionary Tale of Numero Cinco' (episode 94)
Angel is attacked by Wolfram & Hart's aged mail-delivery guy, Numero Cinco, setting in motion a bizarre chain of events that culminates in Angel fighting an Aztec Day of the Dead demon. As bad as it sounds.

31

'Carpe Noctem' (episode 48)
An old man, Marcus, casts a body-swapping spell on Angel. Actually, far *worse* than it sounds.

 'The Ring' (episode 16)
A man hires Angel to investigate the kidnapping of his brother but Angel soon realises that this is a trap to lure him into a demon fight club. Overly bloody and rather boring.

THE GOOD BOOK
Biblical references or allusions in *Angel*

- I Timothy 6:12 ('Hero', 'A Hole in the World', 'Not Fade Away').

- Isaiah 48:22 ('Parting Gifts', 'Not Fade Away').

- I Samuel 17–18 ('Expecting', 'Happy Anniversary').

- Luke 15 ('The Prodigal').

- Matthew 6:9–13 ('The Prodigal').

- Matthew 26 ('To Shanshu in LA', 'Sleep Tight', 'A New World', 'The Magic Bullet', 'Origin', 'Not Fade Away').

- Proverbs 16:18 ('Judgment').

- The Book of Job ('That Vision Thing').

- Genesis 2–3 ('Billy', 'Sleep Tight', 'Conviction', 'Not Fade Away').

- Luke 1–2 ('Lullaby').

- Judges 14 ('Couplet').

- Revelation 8 ('Loyalty').

- Galatians 6:7 ('The Price').

- Judges 15–16 ('Tomorrow').
- Luke 23 ('Calvary').
- Ecclesiastes 3 ('Shiny Happy People').
- John 14 ('Shiny Happy People', 'Peace Out').
- Exodus 21:23 ('Just Rewards', 'Harm's Way').
- Revelation 20 ('Just Rewards', 'Time Bomb').
- Matthew 18:9 ('Destiny').
- Revelation 6 ('Harm's Way').
- Exodus 13 ('Damage').
- Mark 5:9 ('Not Fade Away').
- Exodus 20 ('Not Fade Away').
- 'Live, drink and be merry' is a variant on a phrase found in Ecclesiastes, Isaiah, I Corinthians and Luke ('The Price').

668: THE NEIGHBOUR OF THE BEAST

Those important LA addresses and phone numbers in full

 The initial Angel Investigations office was apartment number 103 of its building – later destroyed in an explosion. Room 101 was occupied by Casas Manufacturing, 104 housed John Folger DDS ('Somnambulist') and 105 was Herbert Stein ('To Shanshu in LA'). The office's telephone number was 555-0162 ('Lonely Heart').

 The Hyperion Hotel was situated at 1481 Hyperion Avenue, Los Angeles, 90036 ('Dear Boy') – although, confusingly, in 'Home' the street number was shown as 4121. It seemingly retained the phone number from the previous office, 213-555-0162 ('Carpe Noctem').

 Cordelia's haunted apartment was #212 Pearson Arms ('Rm W/a Vu'). Later on, the full address was given as 141 Embury St, Apt 212, Silver Lake 90026 ('Judgment'). Her phone number was 323-555-0175.

 Wesley's house number appeared to be 2337 ('Loyalty') and his apartment was #105. An old lady called Mrs Starns resided in the apartment above him ('Epiphany').

Though she lived at the Hyperion for the best part of two years, in 'Smile Time' Fred's current home was said to be at 511 Windwood Circle.

The address of the Wolfram & Hart offices was 1127 Spring Street, Los Angeles, CA90008 ('Conviction').

Anne Steele's address was 5632 Willoughby Avenue, Los Angeles, and she ran the East Hills Teen Centre on Crenshaw Street ('Blood Money').

As teenagers, Charles Gunn and his sister Alonna lived in a shelter on Summer Street ('War Zone'). In 'Judgment' Gunn's latest 'crib' was said to be off 8th Street.

The house where Holtz's army was being trained was situated at 2239 Santa Elena in Silver Lake ('Loyalty').

Holtz and Connor stayed at the French Cottage Motel on West Sunset Boulevard ('Benediction').

The fetish-loving hitman Spanky's address was on Temple Street in Echo Park ('Conviction').

Nina Ash's address – for 25 days out of each 28 – was 2315 Harvard Street ('Unleashed').

Doyle's telephone number was 555-0189 ('Rm W/a Vu').

Wesley and Gunn posted 6,000 flyers around town advertising the services of Angel Investigations ('Provider'). Unfortunately, these mistakenly contained the phone number of Fabrizio's Pizza (213-555-0126).

 The address that Darla and Lindsey used for their set-up of Angel was 1409 Galloway, Studio City ('Dear Boy').

 Although we never got a specific address for Caritas, it appeared to be situated in Chinatown ('Redefinition', 'That Old Gang of Mine') near to a restaurant called *Pung Fat Lucy's*.

 Detective Kate Lockley lived in apartment #311 ('Epiphany').

 Justine Cooper lived at 7221 Spalding Drive in Century City ('Dad').

SCREAM A LITTLE SCREAM FOR ME

Classic horror movies referenced or alluded to in *Angel*

- *Vampire Hunter D* ('City Of').

- *The Hidden* ('Lonely Heart').

- *Alien* ('Lonely Heart', 'Double or Nothing', 'Harm's Way').

- *Poltergeist* ('Rm W/a Vu').

- *End of Days* ('I Will Remember You', 'Hero').

- *Psycho* ('Somnambulist', 'Are You Now or Have You Ever Been?' 'That Old Gang of Mine', 'Hellbound').

- *Rosemary's Baby*, *Village of the Damned*, *I Don't Want to Be Born*, *The Unborn*, *Demon Seed* and *To the Devil ... a Daughter* are all obvious recurring riffs in both 'Excepting' and 'Inside Out'.

- *Carrie* ('She', 'Untouched').

- *The Exorcist* ('I've Got You Under My Skin', 'Apocalypse Nowish', 'Damage').

- *The Bad Seed* ('I've Got You Under My Skin').

- *Fright Night* ('Eternity').

- *Dracula* ('Eternity', 'Are You Now or Have You Ever Been?' 'Sacrifice').

- *Tower of Terror* ('Are You Now or Have You Ever Been?').

- *The Fury* ('Untouched').

- *Firestarter* ('Untouched').

- *Friday the 13th, Part VII – The New Blood* ('Untouched').

- *The Dead Zone* ('Happy Anniversary').

- *Night of the Living Dead* ('The Thin Dead Line', 'Habeas Corpses').

- *Angel Heart* ('Reprise', 'Life of the Party').

- *Sleepy Hollow* ('Epiphany').

- *Coma* ('Dead End').

- *The Masque of the Red Death* ('Over the Rainbow', 'Damage').

- *The Blair Witch Project* ('Through the Looking Glass').

- *The Phantom of the Opera* ('That Vision Thing').

- *Alien: Resurrection* ('Fredless').

- *The Hunger* ('Offspring').

- *The Omen* ('Offspring').

- *C.H.U.D.* ('Quickening').

- *Twins of Evil* ('Quickening').

- *Invasion of the Bodysnatchers* ('Lullaby', 'Players', 'Sacrifice').

- *Twilight Zone: The Movie* ('Loyalty').
- *The Lost Boys* ('Loyalty').
- *The Birds* ('The Price', 'Apocalypse Nowish').
- *The Evil Dead* ('Deep Down').
- *The Fearless Vampire Killers* ('Spin the Bottle').
- *Resident Evil* ('Habeas Corpses', 'Hellbound').
- *Peeping Tom* ('Long Day's Journey').
- *Dracula, Prince of Darkness* ('Orpheus').
- *I Dismember Mama* ('Shiny Happy People').
- *The Stepford Wives* ('Sacrifice').
- *Night of the Comet* ('Peace Out').
- *Frankenstein* ('Unleashed', 'Shells').
- *Society* ('Unleashed').
- *The Vault of Horror* ('Hellbound').
- *Hellraiser* ('Hellbound').
- *Ghost Story* ('Hellbound', 'Power Play').
- *The Wicker Man* ('Life of the Party').
- *Marathon Man* ('Soul Purpose').
- *The Ring* ('Damage').
- *Scream and Scream Again* ('Damage').
- *Sleepy Hollow* ('A Hole in the World').

- Influences on a story about a detached hand with a life of its own ('I Fall to Pieces' and 'Dead End') include *The Addams Family*, *Dr Terror's House of Horror*, *The Hands of Orlac*, *The Beast with Five Fingers* and *Evil Dead 2*.

FIRST SOLDIER DOWN
The life and times of Allen Francis Doyle

Half-human, half-Brachen demon, wholly charming, Doyle was Angel's initial link to The Powers That Be.

 A hard-drinking, hard-gambling Irishman gifted with prophetic visions and cursed with the, accompanying, skull-splitting migraines, Doyle was the heart of the Angel Investigations team when they first set up in business; Angel's guide and friend. After his death, nothing would ever be quite the same again. His was a brief career, but a glorious one.

 Doyle started as he meant to go on, introducing himself to Angel, explaining his mission and then declaring himself parched from all this yakkin' and in need of a beer. However, he soon proved himself to be remarkably insightful, realising both that Angel's isolation would, inevitably, lead to trouble and that Cordelia could be the connection that Angel needed to humanity to give him purpose. Thanks to Doyle, Angel gained exactly what he most needed – companionship.

 Doyle's visions helped the team to identify the hopeless and those most in need. But they were, by no means, an unmixed blessing and seem to have been given to Doyle –

at least partially – as punishment for some unspecified wrongdoing. It seemed that Angel wasn't the only team member who had some atoning to do ('City Of').

When Spike arrived in LA on a mission to torture Angel and steal the Gem of Amara, he was briefly impressed with Doyle's courage. Doyle, meanwhile, put his life on the line for his boss by contacting old acquaintances in an attempt to find information on the visiting vampire's whereabouts. In doing so, he revived memories of sundry unpaid debts. (It would appear that his mission from The Powers That Be did not come with a salary cheque.)

Doyle was excited by the prospect of introducing Angel to sordid-sounding haunts, though as far as Cordelia was concerned few things could be more insalubrious than Doyle's revolting apartment ('In the Dark').

For all Doyle and Cordelia's verbal sparring it was quickly evident that the pair were attracted to one another. Or, at least, that Doyle was attracted to Cordelia and Cordelia wasn't, entirely, repulsed by her colleague. However, Doyle was far too shy to take the plunge and actually ask her on a date. To further complicate matters, Doyle confessed himself to be just a shade attracted to their dark and brooding employer. It was the swirling coat and the air of mystery, seemingly, that did it for him ('I Fall to Pieces').

When Doyle's debts led him into serious danger he turned to Angel for help and was appalled to find a damp and semi-clad Cordelia in Angel's apartment. Jumping to the obvious (and wrong) conclusion he angrily berated his boss for moving in on his girl and not giving a homely little guy a chance. Once the situation was explained, Angel offered to deal with Doyle's demonic debt problem in exchange for Doyle finding Cordelia somewhere else to live before she drove Angel completely crazy.

Sadly, Angel's solution involved Doyle actually paying off his debts. Angel says that he fails to understand why Doyle chooses to live such a dangerous life. Doyle's reply is simple, but telling. It's the kind of life that stops his expectations from ever getting too high. However, it's not all gloom and doom; Cordelia is a definite highlight of his existence. Some day, Doyle promises, he will tell Angel his life story – a glorious tale of taverns, beautiful women with loose morals and of a past that won't let go ('Rm W/a Vu').

As Cordelia regained her confidence and began dating eligible young men, Doyle became increasingly jealous and convinced that he did not stand a chance of winning the girl of his dreams. However, his brooding was interrupted, first by a good fight where, due to his natural sense of fair play, he refused to use his demonic powers to gain an advantage and then by the chance to save a grateful Cordelia from a vampire attack. Cordelia began to see that Doyle had some hidden depth and it seemed that Doyle may have finally been in with a chance.

Sadly, Doyle's former wife Harry chose that exact moment to turn up to spoil the mood. Thereafter, Doyle found himself in need of rescuing from a potentially lethal stag night. Unaware of her new fiancé's plan to eat her ex-husband's brains, Harry filled Angel and Cordelia in on some interesting details concerning Doyle's past life. Cordelia was, frankly, astonished to hear that Doyle was once a teacher and a food bank volunteer, while Angel was somewhat less surprised to discover that his colleague had great difficulty in adjusting to his half-demon status ('The Bachelor Party').

Angel's heroic rejection of humanity ('I Will Remember You') made Doyle question his own failure to tell Cordy about his heritage, but his confession was interrupted by a vision, which led Angel to a group of terrified demons hiding from The Scourge.

Doyle reacted with terror to this news and with very good reason. The last time he encountered The Scourge, his insecurity led him to reject a plea for help from fellow half-breed Brachans. It was for this act of betrayal that he was punished with the first of his visions and by the knowledge that his inaction had contributed to the deaths of many of his kind.

This time it would be very different. Doyle conquered his fear and helped the demons, even going to the extent of bringing back a scared and angry boy who, possibly, reminded Doyle of his own younger self. It seemed that, after all, Angel was right – you never know your own strength until you've been tested.

Once Cordelia learned of Doyle's true nature she berated him for not telling her, noting that being a half-demon was somewhat low on the (long) list of his faults. Well below being short and poor. Then, to Doyle's astonishment, she asked him to take her on a date. But the couple would never have a chance to cement their relationship. The team's plan was betrayed and The Scourge arrived in force, bearing a beacon which, when activated, would destroy all traces of humanity within a quarter-mile radius.

Faced with an impossible situation Doyle behaved like the hero that he had already become. Overruling Angel's suicidal plan to disconnect the beacon by knocking his boss into the hold, Doyle tenderly kissed Cordelia goodbye, revealed his demonic face to her and went to a truly noble death ('Hero').

Doyle was, indeed, a hero; nothing in his life became him like the leaving of it. Such was Doyle's impact on the team that, many years later, Cordelia chose to spend part of her final day on Earth watching a video of her friend. It was Doyle's example that ultimately inspired Angel to keep fighting the good fight ('You're Welcome').

'Is that it? Am I done?'

'THE IDEA OF A VAMPIRE IN A WHITE HAT PROBABLY SEEMS A LITTLE "GIVE ME A BREAK-Y"'

12 classic lines of dialogue from *Angel*'s Season 1

- Doyle: 'I've been sent. By The Powers That Be.' Angel: 'The powers that be *what*?' ('City Of').

- Kate: 'You can go to *Hell*.' Angel: 'Been there, done that' ('Lonely Heart').

- Angel, on *The Cordettes*: 'A bunch of girls from wealthy families. They ruled high school. Decided what was in, who was popular. It was like the Soviet Secret Police. If they cared a lot about shoes' ('Rm W/a Vu').

- Cordelia: 'Am I wrong in thinking that a "Please" and "Thank You" is generally considered good form when requesting a dismemberment?' ('Sense and Sensitivity').

- Barney's advice to Cordelia on overcoming nerves: 'Little trick. Picture everybody ...' Cordelia: 'In their underwear?' Barney: 'I was gonna say dead. But hey, if that underwear thing works for you ...' ('Parting Gift').

- Angel: 'People change.' Penn: 'We're not *people*' ('Somnambulist').

- Cordelia: 'My glamorous LA-life. I get to make the coffee *and* chain the boss to the bed. Gotta join a union' ('Somnambulist').

- Angelus, about to kill the father he hated: 'Strange. Somehow you seemed taller when I was alive ... To think I ever let such a tiny, trembling thing make me feel the way you did' ('The Prodigal').

- Rebecca: 'You're not a killer?' Angel: 'I gave that up.' Rebecca: 'There's a support group for everything in this town, I guess' ('Eternity').

- Lee: 'This is getting ridiculous. The first assassin kills the second assassin, sent to kill the first assassin, who didn't assassinate anyone until we hired the second assassin to assassinate her.' Lindsey: 'This obviously isn't working.' Lilah: 'You *think*?' ('Sanctuary').

- Gunn: 'I don't need advice from some middle-class white dude, that's *dead*' ('War Zone').

- Lilah: 'Aren't we going to be late?' Holland: 'You never want to be on time for a ritual, the chanting, the blood rites, they go one forever.' And, on arriving at the ceremony: 'They haven't even gotten to the *Latin* yet!' ('To Shanshu in LA').

'WEST HOLLYWOOD!'

The 20 gayest moments in *Angel*

The debate in fandom about Angel's sexual orientation was always a fierce one. The *Angel* writers were, seemingly, not oblivious to this. After many fans misheard Doyle's question 'Are you game?' in 'City Of' as 'Are you gay?' several subsequent scripts were apparently used to indulge us with a few 'slash-fiction' fantasies via some of the filthiest innuendo heard this side of *Round the Horne*. Cordelia, of course, mentions that Angel has 'a gay man's taste' when it comes to clothes ('Disharmony') so perhaps we shouldn't be too surprised by such revelations.

'In the Dark'
In Spike's rooftop monologue he considers that Angel uses 'Nancy-Boy hair-gel' and gets his jollies by working up a load of sexual tension then prancing away like a magnificent *pouf*. However, Rachel, it would seem, totally understands. After all, she has a nephew who is gay.

'I Fall to Pieces'
As Doyle waxes lyrically about Angel, Cordelia worries that she may be interrupting a private moment. Doyle quickly denies that he, himself, is attracted to Angel. Then,

49

having seen his boss make a trademark dramatic exit, he modifies. Maybe he is *a little* attracted.

'Judgment'
The Host's assessment of Angel is that he's smart *and cute*. What type of bar is Caritas, anyway? See also, 'Through the Looking Glass', where Lorne describes Angel as gorgeous.

'First Impressions'
When waking Angel from a bad dream, Wesley ends up with Angel lying on top of him. Naked. Wes subsequently, perhaps in retaliation, gives Angel a pink crash helmet to wear. 'Looks good. Hop on, *gorgeous*,' he notes.

'Darla'
Even in 1880, Spike was putting Angel's back up by calling him a poofter.

'Reunion'
Darla tenderly comforts a distraught Drusilla by stroking her hair. An irate bigot, watching them, angrily demands that Darla and her girlfriend take their make-out session somewhere else. His homophobia earns him a rather bloody death.

'Carpe Noctem'
Marcus, who has borrowed Angel's body, is told by Cordelia that he must speak to Fred and nip any blossoming relationship in the bud. Marcus assumes that Fred is male and proceeds to have a rather awkward conversation with the only other man in the building, a highly embarrassed Wesley.

'Waiting in the Wings'
A ballet-themed episode. Clearly suspicious. When asked at a press release whether Angel was gay, co-creator David Greenwalt quipped, 'You've seen the clothes. You tell me.'

'Loyalty'
Wesley and Angel take baby Connor to the clinic and get some understanding looks from staff and patients alike. Well, they *do* make a lovely couple.

'Slouching Towards Bethlehem'
Lorne tells Cordelia that she may find some of her lingerie missing. But that it wasn't for him, it was for a friend.

'Spin the Bottle'
As Wesley and Gunn wrestle for alpha-male supremacy, Cordelia tells them that she isn't impressed by their homo-erotic buddy-cop session. Meanwhile, Angel worries that Cordy may consider him womanish.

'Release'
A girl junkie finds Faith very attractive and asks if she wants to make out.

Season 5
Perhaps the gayest of all years. From 'Just Rewards' – Angel introduces himself as representing Wolfram & Hart and Spike adds, 'I'm his date' – to the handholding in 'A Hole in the World', the writers never missed an opportunity to play up the homoerotic subtext between Angel and Spike. Sadly, due to the series' cancellation we shall never see the *Some Like It Hot*-influenced episode that David Boreanaz intended to pitch for season six.

'Conviction'
Wolfram & Hart's wetworks commander refers to Angel as a 'pathetic little fairy'. A stung Angel replies, simply, that he's not little. Earlier, he has declared to the fetishist assassin Spanky that he has no problem spanking men.

'Hellbound'
Gunn alludes to one of Spike's more disturbing habits: suddenly appearing when Charles is in the men's room and, apparently, commenting about the size of his willy.

'Lineage'
When meeting Roger Wyndam-Pryce for the first time, Lorne notes that it's like Winston Churchill and a young Richard Harris had a beautiful love child. Which, according to Lorne's sources, may not be as ridiculous as it sounds.

'Destiny'
In a flashback scene full of sexual tension and overt S&M allusions, when they are first introduced, Angelus asks William if he has any idea what it's like to have only women as travelling companions. As he does this, Angelus holds William's arm in the sunlight, causing his skin to burn. Angelus continues that he likes the ladies all right but, lately, he's been wondering what it would be like to share the slaughter of innocents with another man.

He then deliberately extends his own arm into the sunlight and, seemingly, enjoys the pain that he experiences. He asks if William believes this makes him some kind of deviant. William, apparently anxious to prove he's equal to the challenge, extends his hand into the sunlight again.

'Damage'
Andrew is deliriously happy that Spike is alive. And more beautiful than ever. Later, Andrew tells Spike that the vampire isn't the only one who's been through a life-changing experience. Giles has trained Andrew to be faster, stronger and 82 per cent more manly than the last time they met. The latter is, definitely, open to debate (although, see 'The Girl in Question').

'Power Play'
Spike tells Illyria that he and Angel have never been intimate. Except possibly once.

'Not Fade Away'
Angel recruits Lindsey for the final fight. 'I want you,' he notes, before confessing that he'd like to rephrase that, something which would clearly make Lindsey more comfortable too.

HELL-A LAW

The sinister machinations of Wolfram & Hart

Welcome to the Home Office.

 At Wolfram & Hart, we understand the needs of the busy world of corporate evil. With a history stretching back to the dawn of time, branches in every major city in this world and a strong inter-dimensional presence, Wolfram & Hart are perfectly placed to deal with all your evil-legal needs.

Our dedicated team of lawyers has access to infinite resources. It's The Senior Partners' pleasure to serve you and to ensure that you will never be convicted of any crime ('City Of'). Remember, we *own* the LAPD ('Harm's Way').

Wolfram & Hart's service is discreet, professional and highly effective. We offer a full range of options, from witness intimidation ('Five by Five') to our ever-popular Internments Acquisitions Department ('Just Rewards'). Our wetworks and clean-up facilities are second to none ('Conviction'). We also employ a team of psychics ('Quickening'), mystics ('Hellbound') and shamans ('Dead End') and own and control a range of holding dimensions ('Underneath'), thus ensuring that we are responsive to the needs of our clientele at all times.

So, whether you want a demon summoned, a vampire reincarnated ('To Shanshu in LA'), an enemy assassinated ('Five by Five'), a dark ritual performed ('Reprise'), a damned relative rescued from Hell ('Billy'), an ex-lover framed for murder ('Dear Boy') or are simply in need of the best unscrupulous legal advice that money can buy, then why not give us a call?

Sign up with us today. You'll be pleasantly surprised by our low prices and complete lack of conscience, ethics or morality. We cater to the living, the dead and all members of the demon community in between.

Call into our luxuriously appointed LA office. A very warm welcome awaits you. In this world ... and the next.

Note:
If you refuse our offer we may be forced to sue you and kill all your children. And, *no one* wants a lawsuit do they ('Judgment')?

Career opportunities
Are you evil? Do you want a long and fulfilling career? Or would you like to subvert our nefarious plans by working from within the belly of the beast? If so, then why not check out the benefits that Wolfram & Hart can offer you?

With our luxurious state-of-the-art facilities and necro-tinted glass, Wolfram & Hart offers a range of options to suit the bright young legal graduate, the go-getting executive, the world-weary hero or the vampire-girl-about-town.

Performance review
In addition to regular appraisals and Christmas purges, the firm is subject to a full external review at 75-year intervals.

Goats will be provided as necessary along with full instructions for the completion of the appropriate ritual sacrifice. All middle managers will be supplied with sacks. Full compliance with visiting Kleynak demons during the review period is expected as a matter of courtesy ('Reprise').

Career advancement

Due to the vagaries of life in an evil multidimensional legal environment you may find yourself facing rapid promotion when all your colleagues are suddenly massacred by rampaging vampires. Please be aware that The Senior Partners take a dim view of employees who neglect to inform the correct authorities of visiting ladies, especially when those ladies end up *eating* the majority of the Contracts Department ('Redefinition'). However, spying on fellow employees is a much-cherished Wolfram & Hart tradition and is *actively encouraged* ('The Price').

Financial regulations

All employees are expected to complete their timesheets accurately ('That Vision Thing') and to contribute to the theft of large sums of money from charitable causes or commit any other such larceny as may be required by the management ('Blood Money').

Disciplinary and grievance procedures

Here at Wolfram & Hart we take matters of discipline very seriously. Letting The Senior Partners down in any way may result in employees being made to eat their own liver ('To Shanshu in LA'). We value loyalty and any attempts to transfer your allegiance to a rival firm will result in your employment being terminated with extreme prejudice ('Blind Date').

The Senior Partners also disapprove of disgruntled ex-employees who attempt to use mystic runes to disguise their covert activities. Culprits may be sucked into a portal and installed in one of our less-pleasant holding dimensions where their hearts will be removed on a daily basis ('Underneath').

Note:
In the event of damage to any Wolfram & Hart holding dimension, the CEO of the branch responsible will be expected to make full reparation to The Senior Partners.

Addendum:
Please be aware that, as of 2004, there is a strict regulation governing the consumption of human blood by employees and the firm has adopted a zero-tolerance policy to the ritual dismemberment of virgins ('Harm's Way').

Employees will also be required to report for reading by the head of our Entertainment Division ('Conviction'). You should consider your choice of song carefully, however, as anything in the Diane Warren *oeuvre* is likely to result in the termination of both your employment and your existence. Except, possibly, 'Rhythm of the Night' ('A Hole in the World').

Day care programme
Our fully trained day care staff will look after your offspring until the day comes when you choose to offer them up as a sacrifice to please The Senior Partners ('Reprise').

Social life
Our annual Halloween office parties are justly renowned ('Life of the Party'). But, sadly, circumstances have forced us to curtail the popular wine-tasting evenings ('Reunion').

Security
The premises are fully protected by zombie guards ('Habeas Corpses'), vampire detectors ('Five by Five'), psychics ('Hellbound') and a very nasty failsafe system in the basement ('You're Welcome'). Should anything or anyone get past these systems, we also have a full team of ultra-violent security guards available for your protection. Mindful of the possibility of computer abuse, Wolfram & Hart offers a secure email system. Ask your line manager for your own personal code-breaking tarantula ('The Price').

Technology
State-of-the-art scientific and medical facilities are matched by a weapons development programme second to none. And, our resource library is out of this world. Literally.

Religious observances
As a non-speciesist multicultural company, we at Wolfram & Hart wish to ensure that all belief systems are respected and catered for. We offer a fully automated 24-hour ritual sacrifice hotline for those occasions when you simply can't get away from your desk to offer up a goat or family member ('Conviction').

Attractive severance package
When it's time for us to part company, we will be more than happy to sever your head ('Blind Date'), your hand ('To Shanshu in LA') or simply send you out to be sliced, diced and returned in two buckets ('Just Rewards'). Alternatively, why not join our spare-parts division and donate your body for the good of the firm ('Dead End').

Full medical benefits
This includes a full range of brain upgrades ('Conviction'), limb re-attachment – evil hands are our speciality – ('Dead End') and sleep and *ennui* removal to keep you at your sparkling best ('Life of the Party').

Death-in-service benefit
Should you be unfortunate enough to die while in our employ and on company premises, our special operative Matthias Pavayne will be delighted to escort your soul to eternal damnation. However, at the discretion of The Senior Partners your mortal form may be resurrected to protect the premises ('Habeas Corpses'). Alternatively, why not become a liaison to The Senior Partners? Don't forget that while your life may – technically – be at an end, your contract extends well beyond that ('Reprise', 'Home'). Our care for our employees is, quite literally, eternal.

Extracts from personnel bulletins

Holland Manners
Former Vice-President of Special Projects, Holland Manners is no longer on this plane of existence. However, he continues to do sterling work at the behest of The Senior Partners. Meanwhile, the position of Special Representative to The Senior Partners is being most ably filled by Nathan Reed.

Gavin Park
Congratulations are due to Gavin on his transfer from the Real Estate Division to Special Projects. With his extensive knowledge of property law and code violations, Gavin has proved an invaluable asset to the firm.

Lindsey McDonald

Mr McDonald joined the firm as a brilliant young graduate and has made rapid progress since. However, some unfortunate scruples of conscience and the acquisition of an (apparently) evil hand have resulted in this employee leaving the company. The Senior Partners are most anxious for any information concerning his whereabouts.

Addenda April 2004:

Lindsey McDonald, having sought to conceal himself from The Senior Partners, was unmasked by the CEO. He subsequently escaped from a holding dimension with the aid of one Illyria. His co-conspirator, Eve, has been relieved of her duties as liaison to The Senior Partners and stripped of her immortality. A warm welcome to her replacement Marcus Hamilton.

Lilah Morgan

Lilah showed an amazing loyalty to the firm, matched by a talent for staying alive; she survived not one but two in-house massacres. However, her enthusiasm for killing Angel rather than simply turning him towards the Dark Side is something of a minus point. As is her liaison with former Watcher Wesley Wyndam-Pryce. Miss Morgan is currently deceased but still firmly under contract to the firm.

Lee Mercer

Unfortunately this employee pursued a personal agenda by hiring rogue Slayer Faith to assassinate Angel. His plan succeeded only in persuading a potentially powerful ally to seek redemption. Moreover, he was found to have been holding talks with rival law firm Klein & Gabler. Mr Mercer's contract was therefore terminated somewhat violently.

Gwen
Gwen's ability to store and instantly recall every record held in Wolfram & Hart's vast database means that, to all intents and purposes, she *is* the Files and Records Department.

Linwood Murrow
Special Representative of The Senior Partners, Linwood failed in his duty to obtain the child of the two vampires for the purposes of dissection. The Senior Partners, however, very definitely approved of his sterling efforts to pin the blame for this fiasco on his colleague Lilah Morgan.

Brad Scott
Former mailroom employee, convicted of embezzling bearer bonds, paroled from Soledad and subsequently *volunteered* his services to the Wolfram & Hart body parts bank.

Personnel update (October 2003)
Following the massacre of all Los Angeles-based Wolfram & Hart employees by The Beast, it has been deemed necessary to undertake an extensive programme of zombie removal, refurbishment and recruitment. Key personnel changes include:

Angel
Our new CEO. Tempted to join our ranks by the promise of a new life for his son, Connor.

Charles Gunn
Escorted to the White Room and shown his full potential. Subsequently given a full brain upgrade by Dr Sparrow.

Wesley Wyndam-Pryce
Unable to resist the possibilities of access to infinite knowledge.

Winifred Burkle
Wolfram & Hart's state-of-the-art science facilities proved an irresistible lure to this brilliant physicist.

Krevlornswath of the Deathwok Clan
Show him a glitzy roster of showbiz names that the company represents and he's *anybody's*.

Rutherford Sirk
Ex-Council of Watchers member. Erudite, British and marvellously deceitful.

Harmony Kendall
Promoted from the typing pool to be Mr Angel's personal assistant.

Knox
Temporary manager of the Science Department, acolyte and potential Qua'ha'xahn to Illyria.

Hauser
Head of Special Operations.

Eve
Liaison to The Senior Partners.

 Note from The Senior Partners
We are aware that the appointment of Angel as CEO of our Los Angeles branch has caused some concern among our

clientele. We would like to take this opportunity to assure you all that this is all part of our long-term planning process and that normal apocalyptic service will be resumed as soon as possible.

In the meantime, contact Ilona at our Rome office and she will be more than delighted to service your every need.

I JUST *LOVE* YOUR ACCENT

15 more-or-less accurate Britishisms in *Angel*

Asked about a perceived British influence in his writing and whether his time in England during the early 1980s and exposure to British telefantasy had scarred him for life, Joss Whedon noted: 'I saw *Blake's 7*, *Sapphire and Steel* and *Doctor Who* but not a great deal. What we watched were our heroes like *Starsky and Hutch* but I watched a huge amount of British TV while I lived in America. That's one of the reasons I was anxious to come.'

 In 'Somnambulist', Wesley says, 'You'd be locked up faster than Lady Hamilton's virtue,' referring to Emily Lyon (1765–1815) the wife of Sir William Hamilton and the lover of Admiral Horatio Nelson.

 Wesley is compared to Hugh Grant, in 'Expecting', an episode in which he's the only English person to use the phrase 'trendy hot spot' since about 1975.

 Wes's prowess at darts is witnessed in both 'Sanctuary' and 'Judgment'. He seems to make a bit of money on the side as a darts hustler – if such a thing exists. Many British fans doubted that a US bar would have a dartboard in it but, as one of the authors can confirm, several British-style pubs (complete with dartboard) are popular with the ex-pat community in the LA area, particularly Ye Olde King's Head in Santa Monica and Robin Hood's in North Hollywood.

In 'The Trial', Cordy says that she thought Wesley was going to be a man and talk to Angel about his obsession with Darla. Wes notes that he *did* ask whether Angel preferred milk or sugar in his tea. This is, he insists, how men talk about things in England.

'Happy Anniversary' is one of Wesley's finest hours, as he turns into a classic Agatha Christie/Dorothy L Sayers-type detective, even getting to perform one of those hackneyed 'here's what *really* happened' scenes straight out of *The Mirror Crack'd* or *Gaudy Night*.

Wesley was always horrified by stories about the Tower of London ('Over the Rainbow'). He's referring to the ancient fortress on the north bank of the Thames. Now a museum, it was a royal residence in the Middle Ages and a notorious jail for many illustrious prisoners who met some grizzly fates there. There's a suggestion that Angel may have spent time imprisoned there, but he's probably just joking.

In 'Offspring', Wes refers to Gunn having 'a snitch' instead of several more British terms for informers, like 'grass' or 'nark'. He's clearly been in California for too long.

When asked about Holtz's beloved England, Sahjhan notes that the country went through a rough patch 60 years ago, but that it's mostly unchanged – warm beer, boiled meat, bad teeth ('Quickening'). A rather typical, uncharitable

American view of various British stereotypes, two of which are mostly inaccurate. At least we've got a National Health Service. And cool bands. And a sense of humour.

 Cordy refers to Wesley as Princess Charles in 'Spin the Bottle'. The teenage Liam hated the British (he calls Wesley an English pig), an attitude that all good Irish Catholic lads of the 1750s would have had towards the foreign invaders.

 In 'Calvary', Angelus notes that Wesley is proper and English and that chicks just *love* a good accent. It makes them all buttery in their nether regions. He adds that he had a bit of an Irish brogue himself and that he'd be happy to use it on Fred when he rapes her to death.

 When Gunn throws a basketball at Wesley in 'Conviction', the latter notes that he prefers cricket. Well, of *course* he does, he's English – it's part of the culture. Actually, it's not hard to imagine Wesley as a decent middle-order batsman, sharp fielder in the covers and with a bit of useful leg-spin in his armoury, plying his trade for some village team in the Cotswolds.

 Spike calls Wesley 'Percy', a crude-but-amusing English euphemism for a penis ('Just Rewards'). Of course, having Spike around suddenly increases the use of English slang expressions a dozenfold. It's so nice to hear a word like 'geezer' casually cropping up in *Angel* as easily as it once did in *Buffy*.

 Andrew's lunch-bag has a Union Jack on it ('Damage'). Spike uses the term 'sack of hammers' to describe Dana's insanity, just as he once did to describe Drusilla in *Buffy*.

This sounds like a plausible cockney slang expression for madness; however, neither *Cassell's Rhyming Slang* nor *The Oxford Dictionary of Slang* feature the phrase.

In 1943, Spike sang a brief – and tuneless – snatch of the then British national anthem, 'God Save the King' ('Why We Fight').

Spike suggests that he and Angel should hit London's West End and take in a show after they save Fred ('A Hole in the World'). Angel notes that he's never seen *Les Miserables*. Spike, seemingly, has and wasn't impressed, implying that halfway through the first act Angel will be considering drinking humans again.

Spike also uses one of his favourite British swear words, bollocks (see *Buffy*: 'The Yoko Factor', 'Real Me', 'Fool for Love', 'Tabula Rasa', 'Wrecked', 'Him', 'Touched'). Additionally, he gives Drogyn the same crude two-fingered up-yours gesture that he once gave to Xander in *Buffy*: 'Hush'. Amusingly, this gesture continues to turn up on lists of 'Obscure Cultural References' on some *Buffy* Internet sites. The probable rationale is that the first historical use of the gesture is often alleged to have been by British – mostly Welsh – longbowmen as an insult to French archers during the battle of Agincourt (1415).

THE CHARISMA SHOW
The fair Cordelia, in all her effervescent glory

For many, even before the cameras started rolling on *Angel*, the main centre of attention wasn't Angel himself, David Boreanaz, but rather his female co-lead. Charisma Carpenter was, for lots of fans, the best reason for watching *Angel*.

 From the moment that she meets her old acquaintance, Angel, at a swanky LA party and asks him, politely, if he's still 'you know … GRRR!' it's clear that moving from Sunnydale to Los Angeles has stripped Cordelia Chase of *none* of the tactless, yet refreshingly straight-talking, attitude that so characterised her time in Buffy's Scooby Gang.

 'It's good to see she's grown as a person,' notes Angel. But Doyle is quick to spot young Cordy's potential as the perfect link to humanity that Angel needs ('City Of'). This trio of misfits then embark on a series of adventures that bond them together – particularly Cordy's acquisition of a haunted apartment ('Rm W/a Vu'). They're then, horribly, torn apart through tragedy ('Hero').

 Doyle's death has a profound effect on Cordelia and, although she develops a close and (usually) friendly working relationship with Wesley – who, let's remember, she once *dated* in Sunnydale – it's a long time before she allows anyone to get as close to her heart as Doyle did.

Being impregnated by a demonic nasty ('Expecting') and twice facing the possibility that Angel has reverted to evil ('Somnambulist', 'Eternity') hardens Cordelia's resolve that the mission she and her friends have embarked upon is the only important thing. This is something that being exposed to the pain of the entire world by Vocah's magic ('To Shanshu in LA') merely reinforces.

Gaining Doyle's visions changes Cordelia but the insight and wisdom that comes with the side-effect headaches are merely another facet of an already impressive arsenal of strengths – notably the street-smart common sense that Cordelia has *always* possessed.

For example, the events of 'First Impressions' show the resourcefulness and bravery of this young woman who has come so far in such a short time. Cordelia saving Veronica's life at the party is one of the great moments of *Angel*; brilliantly underplayed and yet emotionally exact. When Cordy shouts 'she needs a doctor' and then, after a pause, silently mouths 'NOW!' to Gunn, it's the moment where Cordy, once and for all, grows up. Her later conversation with Gunn concerning his self-destructive tendencies is further evidence of this increasing maturity.

'Untouched' also shows two sides of Cordy. She is, and will remain for a long time afterwards, the only person who can get underneath Angel's skin and bring out a less brooding character. When Angel threatens to sack Cordy, she simply tells him that he can't because she is his vision girl. Then, defiantly, she sticks her tongue out. Even Angel can't help but smile at that. Yet at the same time, Cordy is the first to realise that the abused Bethany is, actually, a huge danger to Angel due to his protective instincts.

Cordy resists several temptations to get too close to Angel ('Personal space!' she squawks when a Darla-obsessed Angel starts stroking her hair in 'Dear Boy'). Possibly it's for that reason that Angel's sacking of Wesley, Cordy and Gunn ('Reunion') is a betrayal that Cordy seems to take the hardest of the three.

Cast adrift, the trio are, at first, directionless ('Redefinition'). But Cordy's organisational instincts pull them through the crisis ('Happy Anniversary') and, ultimately, it's the danger that she stumbles into that brings Angel back into the fold ('Epiphany'). Cordy retains her anger at Angel only briefly when his tasteful selection of replacement clothes for her melts her frosty exterior.

The rapid confrontations with her old life ('Disharmony'), her nominal notions of good and bad ('Dead End') and her virtually moribund acting career ('Belonging') culminate in Cordy stumbling through a dimensional portal into Pylea – where she goes from cow slave to princess in no time at all ('Over the Rainbow'). Some people have all the luck.

But Cordy's perception of her own responsibilities has been strengthened by her experiences and she even turns down the opportunity to be rid of her visions to the Groosalugg and sacrifices both love and a potentially easy life because she believes it isn't her destiny to do so ('There's No Place Like Plrtz Glrb').

Back in LA, 'That Vision Thing' sees Cordelia undergoing Job-like torments linked to her power. It's a theme that runs right through this period, culminating in Skip giving her the opportunity to live a different life and leave the visions behind.

It's a tempting offer – in the alternate reality she's a sitcom superstar. But even here, Cordelia feels that something is missing from her life and finds it in the shape of an anguished, insane Angel who took Doyle's visions instead of her ('Birthday'). That Cordelia turns down her fantasy life and elects to retain the visions and all that comes with them – becoming part demon, for one thing – says much about her priorities.

Those priorities are central to a beautiful feminist parable about male aggression and the terrors of being trapped in a cycle of abuse ('Billy'). This includes one of the defining moments in Cordelia's life: when Fred asks her how she can contemplate facing the powerful Billy Blim alone, Cordy simply replies, 'How can I not?'

Cordy is somewhat horrified that Angel impregnated and then abandoned Darla ('Offspring') although, once Connor is born, she is the closest thing that the baby has to a mother ('Dad'). And, when a night at the opera turns supernaturally spooky, her own relationship with Angel suddenly comes sharply into focus – for Angel at least ('Waiting in the Wings').

Cordy, however, is more interested in the arrival from Pylea of Groo ('Couplet'). Once Angel has provided an antidote to the pesky 'loss of visions through intercourse'-

71

thing, Cordy and Groo depart for a well-earned *com-shucking* holiday. And, significantly, it's while Cordelia is gone that Angel and Wesley's lives fall apart.

In the aftermath of her – probably unconscious – attempts to remodel Groo into a surrogate Angel ('Benediction'), it seems that Cordy finally wakes up to reality just as, ironically, she is seemingly chosen for a new mission. One a world or two away from Angel Investigations ('Tomorrow').

However, life as a Higher Being frankly bores Cordy ('Deep Down', 'Ground State', 'The House Always Wins') and, for reasons that neither she nor her friends understand until much later, she returns to reality, albeit with her memories missing. With anything but hilarious consequences ('Slouching Towards Bethlehem').

It's subsequently clear that Lorne's attempted spell to restore Cordy's memories ('Spin the Bottle') unleashes a demonic power that, from then on, uses Cordelia to spread its sinister and nefarious skulduggery.

And what a blessing it is to be able to say that it's not *really* Cordy who sleeps with Connor in one of the most 'ewww'-inducing examples of quasi-incest in television history ('Apocalypse Nowish'). It's also not really Cordy who manipulates Angel into having his soul removed, then stealing it, attempting to kill Willow ('Orpheus') and actually killing Manjet ('Long Day's Journey'), the Svear priestesses ('Soulless') and Lilah ('Calvary').

It's the demon inhabiting Cordelia that directs the actions of The Beast ('Salvage') and persuades Connor to go against all of his instincts and murder an innocent teenage girl to induce the birth of their illegitimate child ('Inside Out').

 Perhaps, during this period, it's best to remember Cordy as the fantasy-girl in Angel's *perfect day* hallucination – back to her smart-alec peak and a tender and gentle lover ('Awakening'). But, of course, it's not real. Angel and Cordelia's relationship remains one of the last great unrequited love stories.

 Her friends finally realise that Cordy is not, exactly, herself ('Players') and Skip reveals that, actually, all the events in Cordy's life since she came to LA have been leading to this point. ('Cordelia was chosen to become a Higher Being because she's sure a pure, radiant saint. *Please!*')

 Having given mystical birth to the Power That Was, Jasmine, Cordelia then spends the next year in a coma and is, understandably, shocked when she wakes up to find that, for instance, Spike is a hero and Angel is CEO of Hell Incorporated; that he employs a soulless vampire like Harmony as his secretary and has, seemingly, been seduced by Wolfram & Hart's schemes and misdirections.

 But Cordy, as Angel eventually discovers, is on one final mission – a special request that The Powers That Be could not refuse her – to save the one person that Angel, seemingly, can't save. Himself ('You're Welcome').

Cordelia's final gift to Angel is a single vision that predicts the steps he and his friends must take to bring down The Circle of the Black Thorn ('Power Play', 'Not Fade Away'). Proving that, even from beyond the grave, Cordelia remains Angel's conscience and his guide.

THERE'S A GHOST IN MY HOUSE
The activities of Cordy's less-than-substantial housemate,
Phantom Dennis

 Poor Dennis Pearson didn't have much of a life. Living with a psychotically jealous mother must have been tough and, when he finally found a nice girl to settle down with, his mother, Maud, didn't take the news well. Indeed, she bricked her errant son in a chimney where he spent the next 54 years watching impotently as his, now–deceased, mother saw off any woman foolish enough to rent the apartment.

 Three apparent suicides later, 212 Pearson Arms is vacant again and Cordelia Chase moves in. Luckily, Maud is no match for the Angel Investigations team or for Cordy herself. Dennis, who up until now has only been able to manifest himself by pressing his face into the wall, is able to mystically alert Cordelia to his plight and – after some quality demolition – Dennis is finally free.

 Cordelia has a new flatmate and Phantom Dennis is happy at last, although Cordy takes a dim view of him moving her drink and changing the channels on the television ('Rm W/a Vu').

Dennis seems to have inherited some of his mother's jealous personality. He is protective of Cordelia and dislikes her having male company. When Cordy arrives home with the seemingly eligible Wilson Christopher, Dennis does everything he can to spoil the mood – turning on the lights and changing Cordelia's romantic mood music to a jaunty polka until an exasperated Cordelia threatens to punish him by playing *Evita* around the clock.

However, Dennis's instincts are proved correct and Wilson turns out to be interested only in impregnating Cordy with his demon seed. The ghost then proves to be a real friend, handing the distraught Cordelia a tissue and tenderly tucking her into bed ('Expecting').

Dennis also shows surprising empathy when Angel, totally out of his depth at a housewarming party, takes refuge in the kitchen. The supportive spook pulls out a chair and passes the unhappy vampire a cold beer ('She').

Gradually, Dennis comes to accept that the Angel Investigations team pose no threat to his relationship with Cordelia – although he seems to have a bit of a problem with Wesley, first refusing to let him enter the apartment until Cordy helpfully informs him that Hell would freeze over before she would have sex with Wes ('Five by Five') and then assisting the ex-Watcher's research by flinging a large book at his head ('Judgment').

For all his attempts at limiting her love life, Cordy has many reasons to be grateful for Dennis's companionship. He may like the apartment at a cooler temperature than is comfortable for humans, but he's great for getting rid of unwanted guests ('That Vision Thing'), fetching telephones ('First Impressions'), adjusting the lighting, organising celebrations ('Birthday'), finding headache tablets and running hot baths. He's also extremely handy with a loofah; in fact, Cordelia wonders how she ever managed without him ('Heartthrob').

Moreover, Dennis is extremely loyal, hiding Cordelia's secrets until persuaded by Gunn that the team need information to help save her life, at which point he reveals Cordy's concealed stash of heavy duty medication ('Birthday').

Sadly, when Cordelia ascends to a higher plane the team can't afford to pay the rent on her home. Dennis – confused and furious after three months alone in an empty, dusty apartment – disrupts the moving process by unpacking Cordelia's possessions as fast as the team can pack them until an exasperated Fred shouts at him that Cordy is not coming back ('Ground State').

It's a sad end to perhaps the brightest period in Dennis's existence. One can only hope that his next flatmate was as accepting of him as Cordelia Chase.

'YOU MAY REMEMBER ME FROM SUCH FILMS AND TV SHOWS AS ...'

15 familiar guest stars on *Angel*

 Despite a long TV career on *Parker Lewis Can't Lose*, *21 Jump Street*, *Friends* and *Ally McBeal*, Kristen Dattilo (Harry in 'The Bachelor Party') remains best remembered for an appearance in Aerosmith's 1990 video 'Janie's Got a Gun'.

 A former ice-skater – once ranked 12th in the US – Julie Benz (Darla) auditioned for the role of Buffy Summers in 1997. She later starred as Kate Topolsky in *Roswell* and in *As Good As It Gets, Jawbreaker, A Fate Totally Worse Than Death, Darkdrive, Shriek if You Know What I Did Last Friday the 13th* and *Satan's School for Girls*.

 Stephanie Romanov (Lilah Morgan) began her career as a model, aged 15, working for *Elle*, *French Vogue* and *Vanity Fair* before moving into acting with the role of Teri Spenser in *Melrose Place* and *Models Inc*. She also appeared in *Due South*, *Spy Hard*, *Tricks* (as Candy), *Sunset Strip* (as Christine) and *Thirteen Days* (as Jackie Kennedy).

Tracy Middendorf (Tina in 'City Of') played Risa Holmes in *Ally McBeal*, Laura Kingman in *Beverly Hills 90210* and Carrie Brady in *Days of Our Lives*. Her guest appearances include *The X-Files*, *Millennium*, *Chicago Hope*, *Star Trek: Deep Space Nine*, *Alias*, *24*, *House* and *The Practice*. 'It seems like I always get cast as emotional women in crisis,' she complained to *TV Guide* in 1999. Still, it's a living, isn't it?

Tony Amendola (Thesulac Demon in 'Are You Now or Have You Ever Been?') plays Bra'tac in *Stargate SG-1*. He was also Sorrel in *Kindred: The Embraced*, Carl Jasper in *Cradle Will Rock* and Sanchez in *Blow* and has appeared in *Charmed*, *Seinfeld*, *Alias*, *The West Wing*, *24* and *She-Wolf of London*.

Gerry Becker (Nathan Reed) was Stanley in *Man on the Moon* and Nixon on *Ally McBeal* and appeared in *Stonewall*, *Hoffa*, *Mickey Blue Eyes* and *Donnie Brasco*.

Daniel Dae Kim (Gavin Park) played John Matheson in *Crusade*, Agent Tom Baker in *24* and Jin in *Lost*. He also featured in *CSI*, *The Jackal* and *Addicted to Love*.

Mississippi-born Gary Grubbs (Roger Burkle) is one of those character actors who seem to have been in *every-thing*. His CV includes *The Astronaut's Wife*, *Will & Grace*, *The X-Files*, *JFK* (as Al Oser), *Foxfire*, *Silkwood*, *Caroline in the City*, *The A-Team*, *The Dukes of Hazzard*, *M*A*S*H*, *The Rockford Files* and *Charlie's Angels*.

Danny Woodburn (Executive Demon in 'The Magic Bullet') played Carl the Gnome in *Special Unit 2* and Head Dwarf in *Charmed*. He also appeared in *Jingle All the Way*, *Sticks* and *CSI*.

Born in Canada in 1980, the daughter of former Huddersfield, Arsenal and England football legend Bob McNab, Mercedes McNab (Harmony Kendall) appeared in *Escape from Atlantis* and *Beer Money*, played the young Sue Storm in *The Fantastic Four* and was Amanda Buckman in *The Addams Family* and *Addams Family Values*. Like numerous teenage actresses, she auditioned for the role of Buffy Summers. Although unsuccessful, along with fellow shortlistees Elizabeth Anne Allen and Julie Benz, she was rewarded with a recurring role in *Buffy* and, subsequently, *Angel*.

Best known for his role as Doctor Phlox in *Enterprise*, John Billingsley (Evan Royce in 'Unleashed') has appeared in *High Crimes*, *The Glass House*, *Crocodile Dundee in Los Angeles*, *Stargate SG-1*, *The Others*, *Kate's Addiction*, *I Love You to Death*, *The West Wing*, *Gilmore Girls*, *Felicity* and *NYPD Blue*.

Christian Kane (Lindsey McDonald) played Wick Lobo on *Rescue 77* and Flyboy Leggat on *Fame LA*. He also appeared in *Just Married* and fronts his own country-rock band, Kane.

A former cheerleader with the San Diego Chargers, Charisma Carpenter (Cordelia Chase) began her acting career in *Baywatch*, playing Hobie's girlfriend Wendie. Aaron Spelling personally auditioned her for the über-vixen-bitch Ashley Green in NBC's *Malibu Shores*. She also played Beth Sullivan in the *Josh Kirby: Time Warrior* TV movies. Subsequent to the seven years she spent on *Buffy* and then *Angel*, she starred as Jane Grant in *See Jane Date* and played Kyra in *Charmed*.

Adam Baldwin (Marcus Hamilton) was the antisocial Jayne Cobb in *Firefly*. His CV also includes appearances in *Betrayal*, *The X-Files*, *Jackpot*, *The Patriot*, *Full Metal Jacket*, *From the Earth to the Moon*, *Poison Ivy*, *The Cape*, *Independence Day* and *Stargate SG-1*.

 Vincent Kartheiser (Connor) has featured in *Dandelion*, *The Unsaid*, *Crime + Punishment in Suburbia*, *Another Day in Paradise* and *Heaven Sent*.

DON'T BE IN THE TEASER

10 reasons why, if you're going to be in an *Angel* episode, you should avoid the pre-title sequence

Supernaturally horrid things happen to Los Angeles residents with alarming regularity in those few moments between the 'Previously on *Angel*' recap and the actual titles. This section lists some of the most memorable.

 Two vampires in the alley: dusted, in spectacular fashion, by Angel ('City Of').

 Slimy demon: killed with magic sword – both of its heads and all its limbs are sliced off and placed in Tupperware containers. ('Sense and Sensitivity').

 Turfog the Slimy Wall Demon: axed by Angel and friends ('Dear Boy').

 Executive: brutally stabs himself in the eye with a carving knife ('Dead End').

 Demon Monks: slaughtered by Angel ('Heartthrob').

Merl: brutally murdered by street vigilantes ('That Old Gang of Mine').

 Young man: reduced to a gooey heap of skin after some rather fantastic sex ('Carpe Noctem').

 Lilah Morgan: beaten to a pulp by Gavin Park ('Billy').

 The Holtz family: a tasty snack for Angelus and Darla ('Quickening').

 Small child: electrocuted by superpowered classmate ('Ground State').

A MAN OF GREAT PROMISE

The fall and rise of Wesley Wyndam-Pryce:
from plank to champion

Wesley is, arguably, the most fascinating character in *Angel*. His transformation from an inept buffonish former Watcher to a tragic hero is a journey that runs the gamut of love, trust, betrayal, revenge and ultimate redemption. In that regard, his story can be seem as a microcosm for the show itself.

 It's something of a game among fans of Joss Whedon's series to name the character who has developed the furthest over the eight years since *Buffy* began. It's true that the journeys made by – for example – Willow, Xander, Cordelia, Spike and Angel have been both long and emotional ones. But let's not forget Wes, a character who in many ways embodies everything that is central to *Buffy* and *Angel* – morality, honesty, nobleness and redemption for past mistakes. Wesley Wyndam-Pryce, one of the *truest* champions in a universe full of them.

 Initially conceived and presented as a character who 'thinks he's Pierce Brosnan but is really George Lazenby', Wesley arrived in Sunnydale full of inappropriately stiff British reserve and clumsy social ineptitude. Not to put too fine a point on it, he's a bit *useless* really. But, even in the early days one sensed Wesley was trying his best and that, when the chips were down, he could usually manage to display a surprising level of bravery.

By the time of his tragic death six years later, Wesley had come a long way. But the basic insecurity of a man bullied by an overbearing father and rejected once too often by his peers was never far from the surface.

Wesley's first appearance in Los Angeles is impressive – a leather-clad figure astride a powerful motorbike chasing a terrified demon. However, Wesley is as ill-at-ease in his role as self-styled 'rogue demon hunter' as he is in his tight-fitting leather trousers. Cast adrift from his calling as a Watcher, Wesley sees himself as a lone wolf. In reality he's lonely and confused, consumed by regret at his abject failure as Faith and Buffy's Watcher. Thus his gratitude at being welcomed into the Angel Investigations organisation is entirely credible ('Parting Gifts').

Wesley's skill with ancient languages and his gift for research are undoubted assets to Angel and Cordelia. However, with money in short supply there's a salary problem, though Cordelia's suggestion that whenever Wesley identifies a demon he receive ten dollars and a chicken pie is met with the scorn it deserves ('Dear Boy').

Nevertheless, as a respected and vital member of the Angel Investigations team Wesley's confidence quickly grows, as do his abilities as a fighter. From a rather timorous man, he evolves into a dangerous adversary with a particular expertise with the crossbow ('The Ring').

However, despite his protestations that he has a rich and varied social life, he is still refreshingly ill at ease in social situations, as witnessed by his admirably uninhibited but *seriously* uncool dancing ('She'). Note, for instance, Cordelia's complete astonishment when Angel reveals that Wesley actually had sex with a bleached-blonde the night before ('Dear Boy').

Wesley's past returns to haunt him in the form of Faith. Newly awakened from her coma and consumed by self-loathing, Faith captures Wesley and subjects him to brutal torture in an attempt to make Angel angry enough to kill her. Wesley displays remarkable strength and courage in this situation and retains enough dignity to counter Faith's cruel goading with a few pithy responses of his own ('Five by Five').

However, Angel's subsequent kindness and concern for Faith both angers and bewilders his injured colleague. When the representatives of the Council of Watchers arrive in LA and offer to reinstate Wesley in return for his help capturing the rogue slayer, Wesley is momentarily tempted. But he realises that he can do more good working with Angel than with the corrupt, bigoted Council ('Sanctuary').

Wesley gets a chance to shine when, in Angel's absence, he assumes the role of his boss in order to protect heiress Virginia Bryce. His impersonation of a vampire is only partially successful and shows that, for all his new-found confidence, he's still capable of tripping over his own feet at the most inappropriate moments. However, his courage and determination are admirable and, in the process of this undercover operation, he both saves the girl *and* is seduced by her. Suddenly, Wesley has a sexy girlfriend and is on the front pages of the society magazines, much to Cordelia's chagrin ('Guise Will Be Guise').

 When Angel fires his team, Wesley is again cast adrift in society ('Reunion'). But his bond with Cordelia and Gunn remains. After a night of maudlin bonding at Caritas ('Redefinition'), the trio decide to go into business on their own, hiring a rather smelly office and continuing to help the helpless ('Blood Money').

 Their initial investigation of a murder mystery involving a rich family is a significant success ('Happy Anniversary'). However, a case involving zombie cops who are persecuting street kids sees Wesley on the receiving end of a bullet meant for Gunn ('The Thin Dead Line'). Virginia is unable to deal with the risks that Wesley's job entails and leaves him ('Reprise').

 Wesley finds himself single again but with the respect and admiration of his colleagues firmly in place ('Epiphany'). Angel, meanwhile, returns to the fold but as employee rather than employer and Wesley is not above taking delight in this turn of events. Atonement is, indeed, a bitch ('Disharmony').

 Wesley befriends Winifred Burkle after the team rescue her from slavery in Pylea ('There's No Place Like Plrtz Glrb') and finds in her a mind even sharper than his own. As Wesley helps her to deal with her traumatic past and to readjust to the world she comes to trust him ('Heartthrob').

Thus, after being infected with misogynistic rage by Billy Blim, Wesley is truly horrified with the darkness and violence that was simmering within him. He shuts himself in his apartment, unable to face the team in general and Fred in particular ('Billy'). Feelings for Fred remain, however, and, gradually, Wesley tries to pluck up the courage to ask her out, only to be beaten to the punch by Gunn ('Waiting in the Wings').

 Sadly, it's Wesley's skill with ancient languages that lead him to one of the darkest periods of his life. Having already successfully translated one prophecy ('To Shanshu in LA'), his research into the Nyasian Scrolls – documents which, he believes, relate to Angel and Connor – bring a hideous revelation. One section translates as 'The father shall kill the son' ('Couplet').

 Wesley is horrified that the signs foretold within the prophecy are coming true. In desperation he tries to remove Connor from danger by kidnapping him, only to play into the hands of the vengeful Daniel Holtz and Justine Cooper. Wesley ends up abandoned in a park with his throat slit, while Holtz takes Connor to Quor-Toth, the darkest of dimensions ('Sleep Tight').

 Assaulted by Angel in his hospital bed and rejected by his friends, Wesley's recuperation is a slow and bitter process. He returns to his apartment, alone and betrayed, clutching a rather pathetic box of belongings. Worse is to come as a depressed Wesley learns from Fred that the prophecy for which he almost gave his life was false ('Double or Nothing').

Wesley tells Gunn that, when he believed he was dying, he fought to live so that he could see his friends again. Thereafter, Lilah Morgan comes to offer Wesley a job with Wolfram & Hart and finds a visibly hardened and bitter man ('A New World'). Wesley angrily rejects Lilah, but the two soon embark on a somewhat tawdry – if extremely passionate – affair ('Tomorrow').

After Angel has been consigned to a watery grave by Connor, Wesley is the one with the resources – both mental and physical – to find and save him. However, it is surely not usual to be having sex with an evil temptress while, simultaneously, keeping the hapless Justine chained up in a closet ('Deep Down').

Having forced Justine to assist him in locating Angel's coffin and released his former friend, Wesley tends to the vampire by feeding him with his own blood before returning him to the Hyperion. Wesley is still alone but has, at least, begun to make reparation for his lapse of judgement.

Wesley gradually rebuilds his links with the team, offering advice to Angel on locating the missing Cordelia ('Ground State') but continuing his disturbing relationship with Lilah ('The House Always Wins'). Thus, he is outraged to discover that the information he passed to Angel was a deliberate mislead on the part of Lilah to enable Wolfram & Hart to gain information from Lorne about The Beast ('Slouching Towards Bethlehem').

Fred is invited to present a paper on physics and Wesley cannot resist attending. When things go terribly wrong Fred is convinced that Angel and Gunn will not help her to seek the vengeance she so desperately needs. So, she turns to Wesley for assistance. ('Supersymmetry').

When Lorne discovers a spell to restore Cordelia's memory, Wesley comes to help and steps into a tense scene between Fred and Gunn. Gunn resents Wesley's intelligence and suspects that Wesley is making a play for his girl. Unable to understand why Wesley is so changed, Gunn asks what happened to the man who once saved Gunn's life. The answer is chillingly simple: 'I had my throat cut and all my friends abandoned me.'

The spell backfires and the participants find themselves regressed to their teenage years, in Wesley's case the bumbling Head Boy of the Watcher's Academy. However, even with all of his idiosyncrasies, young Wyndam-Pryce displays a fair degree of courage and gallantry. It's just a pity that his gaucherie and lack of social skills – particularly where the ladies are concerned – are so *very* annoying ('Spin the Bottle'). Later, as The Beast rampages through LA and the apocalypse approaches, Wesley makes a decision to break up with Lilah. But he also proves that he's far from heartless by saving her life when Wolfram & Hart is overrun by zombies ('Habeas Corpses').

Sadly, Lilah's reprieve doesn't last long, as she's killed by a possessed Cordelia, leaving Wesley under the misapprehension that the resurrected Angelus was responsible and with the horrific task of beheading his former lover ('Salvage'). Later, he tries to explain to Fred about his affair with Lilah. When you are alienated from the people you love, he notes, you start to look in other places ('Players').

The aftermath of Lilah's death is one of Wesley's finest hours as he reacts with moving dignity to the heartbreak of loss. The team desperately need their leader back and Wesley's solution, appropriately, is redemption. He frees Faith from prison ('Salvage') and supports her as she works to save Angel. Wesley tells Faith that it's about choices, the ones that we make and the ones that we don't ('Release').

When Willow arrives to re-ensoul Angel, she describes Wesley as the Marlboro Man's extra-stubbly, mentally unstable, insomniac first cousin. Later the pair talk and Wesley describes how he has seen darkness in himself which he isn't sure that she'd understand. However, when Willow tells him of her own trip to the dark side Wesley concedes that he can't compete with almost destroying the world ('Orpheus').

The divine Jasmine arrives with her message of peace, love, harmony and eating people, and Wesley – along with all of his friends – chooses to worship her. In his case, by developing a website ('The Magic Bullet').

Later, when the Angel Investigations team have – much to their disappointment – ended world peace, Wesley is tempted into joining Wolfram & Hart by the fabulous library of magical resources and, intriguingly, by a staff headed by Rutherford Sirk, a former member of the Watcher's Council. However, unbeknown to Wesley, Angel has made a deal that will wipe out the team's memories of aspects of recent events ('Home').

In Wolfram & Hart, Wesley seems once again to have found a place in the world, despite his misgivings as to the evil nature of the firm ('Conviction'). One thorn in his side, however, is the ebullient Knox, who heads up Fred's science team and is entirely too personable and friendly with Fred for Wesley's comfort.

Despite this, Wesley seems relatively at ease in his new surroundings, although he is deeply concerned about Angel's increasing isolation ('The Cautionary Tale of Numero Cinco'). However, Wesley's old insecurities resurface when he seemingly receives a visit from his father. Wesley is already feeling guilty after Fred was injured during an operation and daddy's presence does nothing to assuage his low self-esteem.

Former Watcher's Council member Roger Wyndam-Pryce is charming to Wesley's colleagues but undermines his son's self-confidence at every opportunity. A few minutes in his presence is enough to reduce Wesley to clumsiness. It should be a relief to Wesley to discover that Roger is, in fact, a cyborg and that, in shooting him to protect Fred, he has not committed patricide. However, a desperately sad phone call to his real father proves that the cyborg was an all too accurate facsimile ('Lineage').

When Wesley and Fred finally begin a relationship, it is tragically short lived as Fred falls victim to the parasitic Illyria. Wesley seems mad with grief, shooting a hapless employee who dares to question the entire company's dedication to finding a cure for Ms Burkle ('A Hole in the World').

After Fred's death, Wesley takes revenge on both Knox and Gunn for their involvement: Gunn is – non-fatally – stabbed and Knox coldly shot – right in the middle of one of Angel's inspiring speeches ('Shells'). Subsequently, Wesley succumbs to a mixture of grief and alcohol before dragging himself back to some form of existence and helping the team in their research on Illyria ('Underneath').

It is Illyria who, unwittingly, reveals that Winifred's memories were altered. Wesley investigates and tracks down Cyvus Vail, ultimately confronting Angel and destroying the Orlon window to restore his own memories. However, through this Wesley gains understanding – that Angel altered the past not to hide the truth but, rather, to be able to endure it.

While a devastated Wesley continues to help Illyria to adapt to this dimension, Angel becomes increasingly concerned by his friend's despair. He tells Wesley that he is needed as part of the team, not drinking himself into a coma and chasing ghosts. Fred is dead, but Wesley is alive and it's about time he started acting like it ('Origin'). Wesley's depression is followed by an intensely manic phase where, as he admits, everything is a bit odd. Despite this he manages to work with Spike to stabilise Illyria and limit her powers ('Time Bomb').

However, it is increasingly clear that Wesley feels isolated and disconnected and, when he falls in the final fight against The Circle of the Black Thorn, he leaves behind a world that has no place for him. Yet he also has a group of close friends who, if they survive, will sorely grieve the loss of a true champion ('Not Fade Away').

THE NOT-SO-SECRET MEANING OF LIFE

The equation in 'Happy Anniversary' that finally solves man's
eternal quest for the secret of time travel

The answer to the question that has baffled Newton, Einstein and
Hawking (among many others) is, according to research physicist
Gene Rainey's blackboard …

$$P = A \left(\frac{\Phi}{2} PX, 9^{17} \frac{C^2}{\Sigma^2}, \frac{V^3}{\Psi} - X \right)$$

$$E^2 = M o^2 C^4 + P^2 C^2$$

Warning:
While reading this book, therefore, it's perfectly possible that
readers may experience strange physical phenomena or, in a worst
case scenario, slip into a different space–time continuum … *We*
certainly did when writing it. At least, that's our excuse.

'SNAKE IN THE WOODSHED'

12 classic lines of dialogue from *Angel's* Season 2

 Gunn, on the Prio Motu: 'Did you find the scumbag that killed him?' Angel: 'I *am* the scumbag that killed him.' ('Judgment')

 Thesulac: 'See what happens when you stick your neck out for them? They throw a rope around it … There is an entire hotel here just full of tortured souls that could really use your help. What do you say?' Angel: 'Take 'em all.' ('Are You Now or Have You Ever Been?')

 Gunn: 'I find Deevak, I'm gonna need more than C3P0 and stick-figure-Barbie backin' me up. No offence.' Wesley: 'Very little taken.' ('First Impressions')

 Darla: 'There's nothing so lovely as dreams … Open those chambers and you can truly understand someone and control them.' Lilah: 'What's hidden in Angel's secret chambers?' Darla: 'Horrors.' ('Untouched')

 Angel: 'Do you love her, Lindsey? Is that what this is? Look at you. A few months with her and you go all schoolboy. I was with her 150 years.' Lindsey: 'But you never loved her.'

Angel: 'I wasn't capable of it. And neither are you.' ('The Trial')

Merl, after Lilah becomes the third person in the episode to attack him in his lair: 'Jeez, does *everyone* know where I live?' ('Blood Money')

Lorne: 'I really can't divulge to you what I read in another being. But I can tell you what I overheard in the men's restroom.' ('Reprise')

Wesley, bursting into Cordelia's apartment to find Harmony painting Cordy's toenails: 'Get away from her ... foot.' ('Disharmony')

Lindsey, when Angel saves his life: 'Why *aren't* you trying to kill me?' ('Dead End')

Lorne, on his world: 'I was there. I came here. I *like* here. I don't wanna go there.' And, when Angel insists that he accompany them to Pylea: 'Remember when I said ... I'm never, never, never gonna leave? Exactly which "never" did you not understand?' ('Over the Rainbow')

Lorne's mother: 'Each morning I go out into the hills where the ground is thorny and parched, beat my breast and curse the loins that gave birth to such a cretinous boy-child ... Your father was right, we ate the wrong son.' ('Through the Looking Glass')

Wesley: 'Should people be bowing in a free society?' Cordelia: 'These things take time.' ('There's No Place Like Plrtz Glrb')

SATURDAY NIGHT AT THE MOVIES ...

Famous – and infamous – films referenced or alluded
to in *Angel*

- *Stardust Memories* ('In the Dark').

- *Ghost* ('Rm V/a Vu', 'Just Rewards').

- *Star Wars Episode 1: The Phantom Menace* ('Sense and Sensitivity', 'Expecting', 'Shiny Happy People').

- *Flash Gordon* ('Sense and Sensitivity', 'Ground State').

- *Clueless* ('Sense and Sensitivity', 'Players').

- *Armageddon* ('Sense and Sensitivity').

- *Gone with the Wind* ('The Bachelor Party', 'Spin the Bottle').

- *A Hard Day's Night* ('The Bachelor Party', 'Shiny Happy People').

- *Titanic* ('I Will Remember You', 'Over the Rainbow').

- *Braveheart* ('Hero').

- *The Man with Two Brains* ('Hero').

- *Mask* ('Hero').

- *Very Bad Things* ('Hero').

- *Star Wars* ('Somnambulist', 'First Impressions', 'That Vision Thing', 'The Price', 'Habeas Corpses', 'Calvary', 'Orpheus', 'Home', 'Soul Purpose').

- *Evita* ('Expecting').

- *Beetlejuice* ('The Ring').

- *The Adventures of Robin Hood* ('The Ring', 'A New World').

- *West Side Story* ('The Ring').

- *Spartacus* ('The Ring').

- *Fight Club* ('The Ring', 'Redefinition').

- *ET – The Extra Terrestrial* ('Eternity').

- *The Wizard of Oz* ('Eternity', 'Belonging', 'Over the Rainbow', 'Through the Looking Glass, 'There's No Place Like Plrtz Glrb', 'Fredless', 'Couplet', 'Spin the Bottle', 'Long Day's Journey', 'Salvage', 'Orpheus', 'Peace Out', 'Just Rewards', 'Soul Purpose', 'Power Play').

- *Do the Right Thing* ('Five by Five').

- *The Naked Truth* ('War Zone').

- *Raiders of the Lost Ark* ('War Zone', 'Quickening', 'Soulless').

- *Pinocchio* ('To Shanshu in LA', 'Hellbound', 'The Cautionary Tale of Numero Cinco', 'Soul Purpose', 'Smile Time', 'Not Fade Away').

- *The Enemy Below* ('Judgment').

- *The Terminator* ('Judgment', 'Billy', 'The Price' 'Benediction', 'Habeas Corpses', 'Underneath').

- *LA Confidential* ('Are You Now or Have You Ever Been? 'First Impressions').

- *Reservoir Dogs* ('First Impressions', 'Dead End', 'Not Fade Away').

- *Malcolm X* ('First Impressions').

- *On the Waterfront* ('Untouched').

- *To Cast a Deadly Spell* ('Guise Will Be Guise').

- *Rocky I, II and III* ('Guise Will Be Guise').

- *Live and Let Die* ('Guise Will Be Guise').

- *Out of Towners* ('Darla').

- *Pulp Fiction* ('Darla, 'Epiphany', 'Quickening', 'Players', 'Origin').

- *All the President's Men* ('The Shroud of Rahmon', 'Conviction').

- *Indiana Jones and the Last Crusade* ('The Trial', 'That Vision Thing', 'Awakening', 'Destiny').

- *The Matrix* ('The Trial', 'Birthday', 'Forgiving', 'A New World', 'Apocalypse Nowish', 'The Cautionary Tale of Numero Cinco', 'Underneath').

- *The Court Jester* ('Reunion').

- *Die Hard* ('Reunion', 'Home', 'Conviction', 'Lineage', 'Not Fade Away').

- *Taxi Driver* ('Redefinition').

- *Godzilla* ('Redefinition').

- *Dirty Harry* ('Blood Money', 'Double or Nothing').

- *Event Horizon* ('Happy Anniversary').

- *Song of the South* ('Reprise').

- *It's a Wonderful Life* ('Epiphany', 'Birthday').

- *The Birdman of Alcatraz* ('Disharmony').

- *48 Hours* ('Dead End').

- *The Empire Strikes Back* ('Dead End', 'Damage').

- *To Die For* ('Belonging').

- *Planet of the Apes* ('Over the Rainbow', 'Time Bomb').

- *Return of the Jedi* ('Over the Rainbow').

- *Monty Python's Holy Grail* ('Over the Rainbow', 'Through the Looking Glass', 'Supersymmetry', 'Inside Out', 'Destiny').

- *Back to the Future* ('Over the Rainbow').

- *Bambi* ('Through the Looking Glass').

- *Mommie Dearest* ('Through the Looking Glass', 'Habeas Corpses').

- *The Elephant Man* ('There's No Place Like Plrtz Glrb', 'That Vision Thing').

- *Home Alone* ('Heartthrob', 'Billy').

- *Field of Dreams* ('Heartthrob').

- *The French Connection* ('Heartthrob', 'Underneath').

- *Lassie* ('That Vision Thing').

- *The Sound of Music* ('That Vision Thing').

- *Magnum Force* ('That Vision Thing').

- *The Usual Suspects* ('That Vision Thing', 'Waiting in the Wings').

- *Thunderball* ('That Vision Thing').

- *Ziegfeld Follies of 1923* ('That Old Gang of Mine')
- *Dead Poets Society* ('Carpe Noctem').
- *Soylent Green* ('Carpe Noctem').
- *The Omega Man* ('Carpe Noctem').
- *Pretty Woman* ('Carpe Noctem').
- *The Godfather, Part III* ('Fredless').
- *Toy Story* ('Quickening').
- *Three Men and a Baby* ('Dad').
- *The Karate Kid* ('Dad').
- *Rio Bravo* ('Dad').
- *Assault on Precinct 13* ('Dad').
- *Gladiator* ('Birthday').
- *Ghostbusters* ('Provider', 'Apocalypse Nowish').
- *The Red Shoes* ('Waiting in the Wings').
- *This is Spinal Tap* ('Waiting in the Wings').
- *Fantasia* ('Waiting in the Wings').

HAPPINESS IS A WARM GUNN

Gangbanger to legal eagle: the turbulent career of Charles Gunn

Charles Gunn is one of the most humane and likeable characters in *Angel*. A streetwise gang leader who once mortgaged his soul to buy a truck ('Double or Nothing'), he would evolve into a key member of the Angel Investigations team. But his sense of intellectual inadequacy would ultimately lead to him making the biggest mistake of his life – a bargain with Wolfram & Hart which, while it releases his potential, eventually will cost the life of one of his best friends.

 Gunn's journey began and seemingly ended in a fight to the death in an alley but, by the time he faces his last battle, he had become a very different man from the brash young vampire hunter whom Angel first encountered.

 Having lived on the streets for most of his life, Gunn's first loyalty was always to his sister Alonna. When she fell victim to a vampire and Charles was forced to stake her, his sense of failure and guilt was overwhelming. He therefore had good reason to hate vampires and was contemptuous of the idea that Angel could be – in any way – 'good'. Nevertheless, he also quickly realised that the vampire with a soul posed no danger to his gang ('War Zone').

As a black man in LA, Gunn was well used to discriminatory attitudes in most walks of life and he channelled these experiences into a viciously funny rant as he provided a distraction, allowing Angel to gain access to Wolfram & Hart. Seemingly, Charles was less outraged by Wolfram & Hart's evil *modus operandi* than by their institutional racism ('Blind Date').

 Initially, Gunn joined the Angel Investigations operation simply as hired muscle, protecting an injured Wesley and Cordelia while Angel was otherwise engaged ('To Shanshu in LA') and striking up an uneasy comradeship with the team ('Are You Now or Have You Ever Been?'). However, when the demon Deevak moves into Gunn's territory, Charles calls in the favour and enlists Angel's help. In the process Charles gains increased respect for Cordelia and Wesley.

 Tellingly, Cordelia has a vision which involves a terrified Gunn and, for all his bluster, it becomes clear that behind the bravado lies a frightened and vulnerable young man, still consumed with guilt over his sister's death ('First Impressions').

 Gunn gradually becomes an established part of the team and is as shocked as his colleagues when Angel fires them all ('Reunion'). Charles quickly finds that returning to his old street life is not an option and, although he insists that his work with Angel was nothing but a side-gig ('Redefinition'), he appears more than happy to join Cordy and Wes as the trio strike out on their own ('Blood Money').

When zombie cops terrorise street kids in Gunn's neighbourhood and Angel is too sunk in his own darkness to care, Gunn turns to Wesley and Cordelia for help. In the ensuing battle, Gunn learns the meaning of true friendship, realising that, while racism is a major issue, the behaviour of many of his former comrades also leaves a lot to be desired. Gunn is initially embarrassed to be seen with a white friend but his attitude changes when Wesley unhesitatingly risks his life, taking a bullet to the stomach to save his new friend ('The Thin Dead Line'). By the time that Angel returns to the fold, Gunn and Wesley have firmly bonded ('Epiphany').

However, their friendship is torn apart when Gunn's old gang lose sight of the mission and embark on a programme of ethnic cleansing of demons, culminating in a lengthy stand-off at Caritas. Gunn initially believes that one rogue member is responsible and conceals incriminating evidence from Wesley, preferring to handle the situation in his own way. By the time he realises his mistake, it's too late. Not only has he placed his friends in serious danger, but he has also lost Wesley's trust ('That Old Gang of Mine').

Worse is to come as both men fall for Winifred Burkle, the beautiful if somewhat barmy physicist whom the team rescue from slavery in Pylea ('Over the Rainbow').

When Angel spends Gunn's money on tickets to the ballet rather than the intended Mahta Hari gig, Gunn is furious. However, in the course of the evening he discovers culture and declares his love to Fred, unwittingly breaking Wesley's heart ('Waiting in the Wings').

Sadly, Gunn later loses Fred's trust when he foils her plan for revenge on the professor who sent her to Pylea. The pair eventually rebuild a relationship as friends and colleagues but never again as lovers ('Supersymmetry'). Perhaps part of the problem is Gunn's continuing sense of intellectual inferiority. Tellingly, when the team revert to their teenage selves, Gunn unhesitatingly identifies his status in the group as merely the muscle ('Spin the Bottle').

 When Wolfram & Hart offer Angel and his friends all the things which they most desire, Gunn sees his opportunity to gain respect and status. Having assumed that he would be assigned to the security department, he is amazed to be escorted instead to the White Room, where a surreal meeting with a panther is, seemingly, a life-changing experience for him. Charles emerges determined to accept Wolfram & Hart's offer ('Home').

 Once ensconced within the evil law firm, Gunn takes advantage of another offer, a potentially dangerous mental upgrade. Gunn, literally overnight, becomes a high-powered legal expert with, as a bonus, an encyclopaedic knowledge of Gilbert and Sullivan's operettas. He now has skills that render him indispensable to the team ('Conviction').

 However, this being Wolfram & Hart, nothing is ever as simple as it seems and Gunn's upgrade proves to be temporary. The evil Dr Sparrow takes pleasure in reminding Gunn that his new-found respect is due – almost entirely – to his recently acquired knowledge. He offers Gunn a deal, one that will have tragic consequences ('Smile Time').

Unbeknown to Gunn, the artefact that he expedites through customs contains the remains of Illyria, an Old One. And Fred, ever curious, cannot resist a closer look at the mysterious sarcophagus ('A Hole in the World').

 As Fred loses her battle for life and Illyria takes over her body, a devastated Gunn cannot bring himself to confess his actions. However, Wesley discovers his secret and, while understanding Gunn not wanting to lose his mental powers, finds that he cannot forgive the withholding of information that may have saved Fred. Wesley brutally stabs his former friend and Gunn is left in the hospital wing to contemplate the price of his betrayal ('Shells').

 Angel tries to convince Gunn that, despite his terrible mistake, he still has much to offer. However, a guilt-stricken Gunn is desperate to make amends and, while on a mission to rescue Lindsey McDonald from a Wolfram & Hart holding dimension, Charles takes the renegade lawyer's place in Hell, submitting to unspeakable torture in a quest for atonement ('Underneath').

 So determined is Gunn to make amends that he nobly rejects Marcus Hamilton's offer to get him out ('Origin'), returning willingly to the torture chamber until he is rescued, fittingly enough, by Illyria ('Time Bomb').

 A sadder and wiser Gunn returns in time to play a full role in the final battle. He takes on seemingly insurmountable odds and, despite Illyria instructing him not to die, he returns from his penultimate mission gravely wounded. Despite this, he stands ready to fight alongside his colleagues, determined to make his last minutes count as the hoards of Hell descend upon them.

Gunn's survival seems unlikely, but he remains loyal to Angel to the last. A flawed man who made mistakes but whose heart was always firmly in the right place ('Not Fade Away').

DREAMING, AS *BUFFY* OFTEN PROVED, IS FREE

Those mind-expanding dream sequences in full

Lots of TV series do cool hallucinatory dream sequences as part of their dramatic *oeuvre*. *Angel*, by contrast, does *magnificent*, surreal, scary, funny ones. You'll find the best of them listed here.

 Angel's sleep is filled with killing dreams. This is worrying for two reasons: first, because Angel finds the dreams enjoyable; second, because they seem to be coming true. Facing the possibility that he has reverted to his old ways, Angel is relieved when investigations prove that the killer is Penn, an apt pupil whom Angel sired in the eighteenth century. ('Somnambulist').

 Renegade Slayer Faith dreams of violently killing Angel. That girl clearly has some freaky stuff going on in her head ('Sanctuary').

 Unaware that Wolfram & Hart have brought Darla back as a human ('To Shanshu in LA') Angel can't understand why his dreams are suddenly filled with erotic images of his sire. Wesley and Cordelia become increasingly concerned as Angel spends most of his time asleep, but when he can moonbathe and dance with Darla, who can blame him ('First Impressions')?

Angel continues to dream of literal bodice-ripping action with Darla, who turns out to be actually in his room and controlling his dreams with Calynthia powder ('Untouched'). Finally, as Angel dreams of his first sighting of Drusilla in 1860, he encounters a very real Darla who leads him into a trap ('Dear Boy').

As Wesley fears an ancient prophecy is coming true and that Connor's life is in danger, he has a terrifying nightmare about Angel killing Connor while Wesley watches, with blood on his own hands ('Loyalty').

In highly impressive contrast to the dark and troublesome dreams of her colleagues, Cordelia notes in 'She' that Wesley awoke her from a seemingly *lovely* shopping dream concerning a 'Going Out of Business' sale at Neiman-Marcus.

Locked in a steel box and sunk to the ocean floor, a starving Angel hallucinates a number of scenarios: these include pure wish-fulfilment (a dinner with all his friends during which Angel is unable to get any food), a romantic encounter with Cordelia (which ends with him siring her) and a shared battle with Connor that culminates in Angel killing his son ('Deep Down').

When the team require the services of Angelus, Angel is magically provided with an elaborate fantasy day in which he seeks and finds reconciliation with all of his friends, and specifically Connor, finds the sword of Bosh M'ad, kills

The Beast and ends up in bed with Cordelia. Unsurprisingly all of this renders him perfectly happy ('Awakening').

Faith and Angelus take a drugged trip into the past century of Angel's life, reliving sundry sartorial disasters, the rescue of a puppy, a lot of misery, some very dubious tastes in music and, crucially, a lapse into drinking human blood that sent Angel spiralling into decades of guilt ('Orpheus').

The day after being bitten by a werewolf, Nina Ash has a horrific waking dream of slashing the throat of her niece, Amanda ('Unleashed').

The incorporeal Spike suffers a series of visions – a woman with no arms, another with a jagged piece of glass sticking out of her eye, a hanged man and a man cutting off his own fingers, all seemingly deceased Wolfram & Hart employees. Believing them, at first, to be ghosts like himself, Spike eventually realises that they are illusions created by The Reaper ('Hellbound').

Under the influence of a parasite, Angel's dreams take an odder turn than usual as he subconsciously questions his destiny and his friends' perceptions of him. In this nightmarish version of reality Spike drinks from the Cup Of Perpetual Torment and gains the reward of Shanshu while Angel crumbles, agonisingly, into dust.

Wesley tells Angel that the vampire has become irrelevant and Spike's arrival has made getting rid of him easier. Then, he stakes Angel.

Fred, assisted by Bear, conducts a bizarre and revealing autopsy on – a very much alive and conscious – Angel.

Worst of all, Spike single-handedly ends Armageddon and turns the world into a beautiful, happily-ever-after, candy-mountain place. He is then rewarded with the love and admiration of all and by a visit from the Blue Fairy, who turns him into a real boy. Angel, meanwhile, becomes a shuffling mailman wearing a very bad tie.

Angel cannot even get an opinion from Lorne since he has no voice to sing with. Lorne does, however, point out repeatedly that Angel has something on his shirt.

Angel manages to remove the parasite only for Eve to replace it with a larger one. Angel then finds himself in a comfy chair sitting in the sunshine with his friends. He is told that he can stay there for as long as he likes. All he has to do is stop caring. At this point, Spike arrives and rips the parasite from Angel's chest, saving him from lapsing into a permanent vegetative state ('Soul Purpose').

When a deranged teenage girl escapes from an LA psychiatric ward, carnage ensues. Dana is a proto-Slayer and, like all of the other Chosen Ones, she has the ability to share the memories of former Slayers. Dana's dreams mistakenly identify Spike as the vampire that killed her family and tortured her into insanity, with devastating results ('Damage').

A drunk and grieving Wesley dreams of himself sitting in a chair with Fred by his side. She asks him to tell her a joke, which he does, although it loses a lot in the translation.

Fred tells Wesley that this is only the first layer and asks if he doesn't want to know how deep she goes. At this point, Wesley awakes to find himself watched over by a baffled Illyria, who is less than impressed by his behaviour or his nightmares ('Underneath').

'THE PLAY'S THE THING ...'

Classic theatrical and literature references or allusions
in *Angel*

- Patricia McLachlin's *Sarah, Plain and Tall* ('Lonely Heart').
- Frank McCourt's *Angela's Ashes* ('In the Dark').
- *Hamlet* ('In the Dark', 'Belonging', 'Forgiving', 'Release', 'Underneath').
- Walter Scott's *Flodden Field* ('I Fall to Pieces').
- Jane Austen's *Sense and Sensibility* ('Sense and Sensitivity').
- Alfred Lord Tennyson's *In Memoriam* ('Hero').
- *Macbeth* ('Parting Gifts', 'Dad', 'Couplet', 'Calvary', 'Home').
- *The Frog Prince* ('Parting Gifts').
- *The Histories of Herodotus* ('Parting Gifts').
- Stephen King's *Apt Pupil* ('Somnambulist'), *The Shining* ('Are You Now or Have You Ever Been?') and *Needful Things* ('Double or Nothing').
- H Rider Haggard's *She* ('She').

- Evelyn Waugh's *A Handful of Dust* ('I've Got You Under My Skin').

- Alexander Pope's *An Essay on Criticism* ('The Prodigal').

- Henrik Ibsen's *A Doll's House* ('Eternity').

- *Tantra Six of Tirumantiram* ('Blind Date').

- Arthur Miller's *The Crucible* ('Are You Now or Have You Ever Been?').

- Charles Dickens's *A Christmas Carol* ('Untouched', 'Orpheus').

- *King Lear* ('Untouched', 'Double or Nothing').

- Anne Rice's *The Vampire Lestat* ('Darla', 'Tomorrow') and *Interview with the Vampire* ('Lullaby').

- Peter S Beagle's *The Last Unicorn* ('Darla').

- WB Yeats's *The Second Coming* ('The Trial', 'Slouching Towards Bethlehem') and *The Circus Animals' Desertion* ('Soulless').

- PG Wodehouse's Bertie Wooster stories ('The Trial', 'The Girl in Question').

- James Jones's *The Thin Red Line* ('The Thin Dead Line').

- HP Lovecraft's *Herbert West – Reanimator* ('Dead End').

- JK Rowling's Harry Potter novels ('Belonging', 'Lineage').

- Lewis Carroll's *Alice's Adventures in Wonderland* ('Through the Looking Glass', 'Fredless', 'Tomorrow').

- *Romeo and Juliet* ('Heartthrob', 'A Hole in the World').

- Dante's *The Divine Comedy* ('Birthday', 'A New World').

- Rudyard Kipling's *If* ('Provider').

- L Ron Hubbard's *Battlefield Earth* ('Couplet').

- Tolkein's *The Lord of the Rings* ('Couplet', 'The Magic Bullet').

- Douglas Adams's *The Hitch-Hiker's Guide to the Galaxy* ('Loyalty').

- *Julius Caesar* ('Sleep Tight', 'Life of the Party', 'The Cautionary Tale of Numero Cinco').

- Henry Longfellow's *Wreck of the Hesperus* ('Sleep Tight').

- Christopher Marlowe's *Dr Faustus* ('Double or Nothing').

- Goethe's *Faust* ('Double or Nothing').

- Robert Heinlein's *The Puppet Masters* ('The Price') and *Stranger in a Strange Land* ('A New World').

- Aldous Huxley's *Brave New World* ('A New World').

- JM Barrie's *Peter Pan* ('A New World').

- Mark Twain's *The Adventures of Tom Sawyer and Huckleberry Finn* ('Tomorrow').

- Ron E Howard's *Conan, the Barbarian* ('Deep Down').

- The Marquis de Sade's *Justine* ('Deep Down').

- Herman Melville's *Moby Dick* ('Deep Down').

- Frederick Kohner's *Gidget* ('Supersymmetry').

- Eugene O'Neill's *Long Day's Journey into Night* ('Long Day's Journey').

- *Othello* ('Soulless').

115

- Sophocles' *Oedipus Rex* ('Soulless').

- Jerry Stahl's *Permanent Midnight* ('Soulless').

- Samuel Taylor Coleridge's *The Rime of the Ancient Mariner* ('Soulless').

- Eleanor Hodgman Porter's *Pollyanna* ('Calvary').

- Somerset Maugham's *The Razor's Edge* ('Salvage').

- Dylan Thomas's *Do Not Go Gentle into That Good Night* ('Orpheus').

- William Cowper's *Olney Hymns* ('Inside Out').

- William Rice Burroughs's *Tarzan* ('Inside Out').

- Elizabeth Barrett Browning's *Sonnets from the Portuguese* ('The Magic Bullet').

- Percy Shelley's *The Mask of Anarchy* ('Sacrifice').

- James Tilton's *Lost Horizon* ('Sacrifice').

- John Donne's *Devotions* ('Peace Out').

- Roald Dahl's *Charlie and the Chocolate Factory* ('Home', 'Power Play').

- EM Forster's *A Room with a View* ('Unleashed').

- Ayn Rand's *Atlas Shrugged* ('Unleashed').

- John Steinbeck's *The Grapes of Wrath* ('Life of the Party').

- Thomas Pynchon's *The Crying of Lot 49* ('Harm's Way').

- George Orwell's *1984* ('Soul Purpose') and *Animal Farm* ('Not Fade Away').

- Pierre de LaClos's *Les Liaisons Dangereuses* ('Why We Fight').

- Jules Verne's *20,000 Leagues under the Sea* ('Why We Fight').

- Daniel Keyes's *Flowers for Algernon* ('Smile Time').

- Frances Hodgson Burnett's *The Little Princess* ('A Hole in the World').

- *The Merchant of Venice* ('Shells').

- *The History of Ali Baba and the 40 Thieves* ('Origin').

- Robbie Burns's *Man Was Made to Mourn* ('Power Play').

THE SINGER, NOT THE SONG
Lorne's finest moments behind the microphone

Krevlornswath of the Deathwok Clan may have been a terrible disappointment to his bearded mother in Pylea but, in Los Angeles, his amazing voice and talent for reading the futures of his karaoke-singing customers made him a huge hit.

It's true that his beloved club, Caritas, had a nasty habit of being blown up and that, in his role as The Host, he had to put up with pretty horrendous mangling of popular songs by some of his clientele. But, whatever the circumstances, the green empath demon strolled through life with a song on his lips and a snappy suit on his back.

Here are some of his finest moments and a plug for his debut CD *Songs for the Love, Lorne*.

 Lorne's first appearance is onstage at Caritas, belting out a spirited rendition of Gloria Gaynor's 'I Will Survive'. As an anagogic demon, The Host offers a valuable service to his clientele, but his cheerful disposition seems to piss Angel off no end. Angel's own rendition of Barry Manilow's 'Mandy' leads Lorne to characterise the broody vampire as a big sap ('Judgment').

Seemingly forgiving Angel for his – allegedly awful – medley of 'Send in the Clowns' and 'Tears of a Clown', Lorne appears in one of Angel's less-fevered dreams about Darla, singing a luscious version of Oleta Adams's torch-song 'Get Here' ('First Impressions').

 Turning from dreams to thoughts of an altogether more fleshy nature, Lorne delivers a memorable version of LaBelle's bordello classic 'Lady Marmalade (Voulez-Vous Coucher Avec Moi, Ce Soir?)' to an enthusiastic Caritas crowd. He also dispenses much needed alcohol to the maudlin former employees of Angel Investigations ('Redefinition').

 In patriotic mood, The Host uses a heartfelt performance of 'The Star Spangled Banner' to wake Angel up when Lorne needs his help urgently and also to test out the acoustics of the Hyperion. Lorne then teams up with Angel to prevent a jilted scientist from destroying the world ('Happy Anniversary').

 As Caritas, apparently, moves from a strictly *Demons Only* door policy towards a more diverse clientele, Lorne sings a glorious interpretation of Douglass Cross and George Cory's '(I Left My Heart in) San Francisco' to an appreciative audience ('Heartthrob').

 Lorne is, understandably, concerned when a gentle crooning of Smokey Robinson's 'Ohh, Baby Baby' fails to soothe the cranky infant Connor. This prompts Lorne to ask Angel if he is absolutely *certain* this child has a soul ('Dad').

119

Perhaps unsurprisingly, Lorne's later – rather wordy – attempt at a lullaby contains pointed references to selling Connor to the first vampire cult who makes him a decent offer ('Waiting in the Wings').

Other Motown highlights include a searing version of Stevie Wonder's 'Superstition' ('Belonging') and the diversionary use of Holland, Dozier and Holland's 'Stop! In the Name of Love' as an escape tool in Pylea ('Over the Rainbow').

It was, perhaps, inevitable that a singer as talented as Lorne would end up starring in his own Vegas show. Despite the fact that he's being held prisoner and forced to assist in the stealing of various people's destinies, Lorne seizes the opportunity to put on a show – albeit a somewhat overproduced one. But, his audience are more than delighted with his outstanding delivery of Kermit the Frog's theme song 'Bein' Green' and his *piece de resistance*, 'Lady Marmalade' ('The House Always Wins').

While narrating the sad-yet-amusing tale of the consequences of a spell that backfired, Lorne sings Marvin Hamlisch's easy-listening standard 'The Way We Were' ('Spin the Bottle').

Keeping vigil at the bedside of the wounded Faith, Lorne sings a snatch from Jimmy Webb's 'MacArthur Park'. Given Faith's drug-addled state, this seems entirely appropriate ('Orpheus').

Unable to resist examining the acoustics of Wolfram & Hart's lobby, Lorne, soon to be head of the Entertainment Division, belts out a celebratory chorus of Leonard

Bernstein's 'Something's Coming' from *West Side Story*. Lorne is, seemingly, astonished that Wolfram & Hart's entertainments roster includes every celebrity he's ever wanted to meet ('Home').

At Wolfram & Hart's Halloween party a sleep-deprived and unstable Lorne sings Thelma Houston's disco classic 'Don't Leave Me This Way'. Lorne's determination to make the party a success leads to disaster as he unwittingly influences his colleagues to obey his every suggestion ('Life of the Party').

When the team are facing the end of the line, Angel tells his friends to enjoy what may be their last day on Earth. It's perhaps inevitable that Lorne heads straight for a stage, a microphone and an audience, giving the performance of his life – a bittersweet rendition of Leslie Bricusse and Cyril Ornadel's 'If I Ruled the World'. A fitting swansong, Lorne leaves the stage and prepares for one final – unpleasant – job, shooting Lindsey with shockingly calm determination before fading out of Angel's life for the last time ('Not Fade Away').

LOVE VIGILANTES

The complexities of standing in the shadows of love with
the Angel Investigations gang

When people work closely together, romance often follows. Angel
Investigations was no exception to the average office situation.
There were dalliances, flirtations and, admittedly, the odd bout of
intense magical sex. But, above all, there were deep, loving and
almost invariably painful relationships.

In the opening episode, Angel expresses his opinion that women
are soft and comfy but that, ultimately, they'll stick a fork in your
heart. He has a point; liaisons in *Angel* rarely seem to end happily
for anyone concerned. Here are some of the most important.

Doyle and Cordelia
Although sent by The Powers That Be to assist Angel,
Doyle is instantly attracted to Cordy. Lust, however, soon
turns to something deeper and a nervous Doyle finds himself trying to pluck up the courage to ask the object of his
affections out on a date ('City Of').

Complications arise in the form of Doyle's (for now secret)
half-demon nature, his ex-wife ('The Bachelor Party'), his
colourful past ('In the Dark') and, most seriously,

Cordelia's declared intention to never again date a 'fixer upper' after the breakdown of her long-term relationship with Xander Harris back in Sunnydale.

However, faced with a life-threatening situation, Doyle finally confesses both his demonic nature and his love for Cordelia and leaves her with a parting kiss as he goes to a heroic and untimely death ('Hero').

Cordelia sincerely mourns Doyle but is less than pleased to discover that his kiss was not simply a sweet farewell but, additionally, a means of gifting her with his skull-splitting visions from The Powers That Be ('Parting Gifts').

Angel and Buffy

When a pissed-off Buffy Summers visits Angel in LA, their reunion is interrupted by a Mohra demon whose blood – in some unspecified way – restores Angel's humanity ('I Will Remember You').

The pair then share one perfect day as they rediscover their love for each other and Angel savours the delights of cookie-dough-fudge-mint-chip ice cream, crunchy peanut butter and the pleasures of the flesh. Sadly, one fight convinces Angel that he cannot protect Buffy as a human and he asks The Oracles to fold back time, leaving him alone with the knowledge of what might have been.

Wesley and Virginia

Wesley meets the beautiful heiress Virginia Bryce while on a mission to protect her *and* while disguised as Angel. Virginia's father chose Angel for this task, believing that Angel's curse would ensure his daughter retained her purity

('Guise Will Be Guise'). Since Angel is off visiting a swami, and the team badly need a paying client, Wesley assumes his boss's identity.

In one respect this plan is less than effective (Wesley struggles to convincingly portray an ultraviolent vampire). However, his disguise brings some interesting fringe benefits since the innocent Virginia turns out to be anything but. As Cordelia notes with some jealousy, after just *one day* as Angel, Wesley is 'getting some'.

When the gang foil Virginia's father's plot to sacrifice her to the goddess Yeska, Wesley and Virginia become a couple but their relationship ends after he is shot ('The Thin Dead Line'), Virginia noting that she can deal with supernatural stuff but seeing Wesley hurt is too much for her to bear ('Reprise').

Angel and Darla

Angel believed that when he staked his sire Darla in Sunnydale, their relationship, which began back in 1752, was finally over. He reckoned without the machinations of Wolfram & Hart, which bring a (now very human) Darla back from Hell ('To Shanshu in LA').

Darla visits Angel's bedroom, using Calynthia powder to keep him asleep while she bestows disturbingly erotic dreams upon him. Angel soon finds himself brooding about his lost love ('First Impressions').

However, Wolfram & Hart's plan seems doomed to failure from the start. Darla, dying of a syphilitic heart condition, is desperate for Angel to restore her to her vampire status

('Darla'). Angel refuses and fights for a second chance for his once-beloved. When this fails he decides to stay with Darla and protect her until her inevitable death ('The Trial').

Wolfram & Hart have other ideas and bring Drusilla to Los Angeles to sire Darla. Angel, unable to prevent this, turns to the dark side, first trying to kill and then, ultimately, sleeping with Darla and experiencing an epiphany of perfect despair ('Reprise').

The consequences of his actions are far reaching, however. Darla, impossibly, becomes pregnant and, influenced by the soul of her unborn child, stakes herself – in the process of giving birth to Connor, Angel's son ('Lullaby').

Angel and Cordelia

Angel and Cordelia fight the good fight side by side and the depth of their feelings for each other is clearly evident. Cordelia is Angel's link to humanity, his confidante. She may mock his brooding moods and deplete the company's accounts with her extravagant tastes in clothes and sushi, but she is essential to Angel, not just as a conduit to The Powers That Be but also as a close and trusted friend. However, their story will ultimately become a tale of missed opportunities and thwarted destiny.

An evening at the ballet seems set to finally lead to a declaration of love when Angel and Cordelia find themselves possessed by the spirits of unrequited lovers ('Waiting in the Wings'). However, the romantic mood is destroyed when an unexpected guest arrives at the Hyperion in the shape of Cordelia's Pylean suitor, the Groosalugg. Angel finds himself nobly putting aside his own feelings to enable Cordelia to consummate her romance ('Couplet').

When Angel and Cordy finally arrange to meet and discuss their relationship, fate takes another cruel twist as Cordelia is sent a message from The Powers That Be; then, escorted by Skip, she ascends to her destiny as a Higher Being. Connor, meanwhile, ambushes Angel and – assisted by Justine – locks him in a steel coffin and sinks him to the bottom of the ocean. The lovers are thus parted, seemingly forever ('Tomorrow').

Rescued by Wesley, Angel searches for his lost love but is persuaded that she is happy in her new role. In reality Cordelia is bored out of her mind and rages, impotently, at Angel's stupidity ('Ground State', 'The House Always Wins').

When Cordelia *does* return, she has no memory of their prior relationship and is terrified by her strange new surroundings. The team's attempts to conceal their unconventional natures and lifestyle only add to her terror ('Slouching Towards Bethlehem').

Searching for her lost past, Cordelia asks the ultimate question, 'Were we in love?' Angel admits that they were.

When Angel is given a fantasy day, it includes Cordelia telling him that his past is unimportant and that only his good deeds matter. They then consummate their relationship. But sadly this is all an illusion designed to give Angel the moment of perfect happiness that is required to remove his soul and restore Angelus ('Awakening').

When it is revealed that Cordelia has become evil and is in league with The Beast, Angel is forced to attempt to kill the woman he loves in order to save the world. But he's unable to carry out this plan before Cordelia gives birth to the divine Jasmine ('Inside Out'). Cordy then falls into a coma ('Shiny Happy People').

Angel's contract with Wolfram & Hart ensures that Cordelia receives the best of medical care, but he grieves for her and is lost without her counsel ('Home').

Disillusioned with Wolfram & Hart's negotiations with evil, Angel threatens to resign his position. At which point Cordelia emerges from a year in her coma with a vision from The Powers That Be and a mission to save Angel from himself. Angel is delighted to have his friend back. But, for Cordy, this is a one-time mission ('You're Welcome').

Like Doyle, Cordy leaves – with a kiss – to do the right thing, even if it isn't the *easy* thing. And Angel is, once again, alone.

Cordelia and the Groosalugg
In Lorne's home dimension of Pylea, Cordelia's visions elevate her from the status of cow-slave to princess. Though she quickly discovers that she's nothing more than a figurehead monarch, she is happy to meet her handsome half-human champion, the Groosalugg, with whom she is, apparently, expected to *com-shuck* ('Over the Rainbow').

When Cordelia leaves Pylea, the Groosalugg tries to govern as an enlightened ruler but he becomes disillusioned and eventually follows his princess to Los Angeles ('Waiting in the Wings').

Cordelia is delighted to see her handsome champion but worries that any consummation of the relationship will lead to the loss of her visions. Angel is forced to help Cordelia find a magical prophylactic ('Couplet').

But it seems that Cordy is conflicted about her love life as she cuts Groo's hair and restyles him, effectively turning him into a clone of Angel. Finally, the Groosalugg realises that Cordelia loves Angel and not him and nobly leaves, his destination unknown ('Tomorrow').

Cordelia and Connor

Cordelia returns from a higher plane of existence in a confused and amnesiac condition and seeks protection from Connor, who seems to be the only halfway normal person around the Hyperion ('Slouching Towards Bethlehem').

Believing that the world is about to end, and regretting that Connor has missed out on many things in his life (and is still a virgin), Cordy lies back and, ahem, gives herself to him ('Apocalypse Nowish').

Angel, unbeknown to the couple, is watching and is, understandably, disturbed by the sight of the love of his life sleeping with his teenaged son. When Cordelia returns to the hotel Angel tells her to take her new boyfriend and get the hell out ('Habeas Corpses').

Once Angelus returns, he asks Connor if it doesn't freak him out knowing that Cordelia used to change his nappies. In effect, the first woman that Connor slept with is the closest thing that he ever had to a mother. On top of which,

Connor has already tried to kill his father. 'There should be a play,' Angelus dryly remarks ('Soulless').

Worse is to come when Cordelia informs a shocked and stunned Angel Investigations team that she is pregnant ('Release'). When the team subsequently discover that Cordelia has been working for the dark side, Connor dramatically rescues her and takes her into hiding ('Inside Out').

Cordy then enlists Connor's help in obtaining the ingredients required for a protective ritual, which include the blood of a young girl. As her and Connor's child is born, Cordelia falls into a coma. Meanwhile, their 'daughter', Jasmine, begins an attempt to enslave the world through peace and love ('Shiny Happy People').

Wesley and Lilah

Abandoned by his friends after an attempt to thwart a false prophecy leads to the abduction of Angel's son, a wounded Wesley begins a rather sordid sexual affair with Lilah Morgan, channelling all his pain, frustration and hate into it ('Tomorrow').

Lilah is well aware of Wesley's feelings towards Fred and cruelly impersonates a Fred-like schoolgirl. Wesley, equally cruelly, insists that she keeps the disguise on throughout their subsequent erotic encounter ('Apocalypse Nowish').

Wesley protects Lilah after she is wounded during The Beast's attack on Wolfram & Hart ('Habeas Corpses') and, when Lilah is killed – seemingly at the hands of Angelus – Wes decapitates her to prevent her from rising as a vampire. A grieving Wesley holds a lengthy conversation with the dead Lilah, admitting that he hoped he could help her to find redemption but that he failed to save her from her own darkness ('Salvage').

He later attempts to save a resurrected Lilah from her contract with Wolfram & Hart and is distressed to find that the contract is, like its terms and conditions, literally eternal ('Home').

Fred and Gunn
Although Winifred had a crush on Angel ('Through the Looking Glass'), it's clear that both Wesley and Gunn develop strong feelings for her. Ultimately, it's Gunn who acts first ('Waiting in the Wings') and the couple are soon enjoying breakfast together and sharing a room at the Hyperion ('Couplet').

When Fred has a physics paper published, Gunn is delighted to support her and attend the conference where Fred will deliver her treatise ('Supersymmetry'). However, an inter-dimensional portal opens and Fred narrowly escapes being transported through it.

Finding that her old professor has been using portals to get rid of his most promising students, and that he was responsible for her nightmare experience in Pylea, Fred seeks revenge. To save his lover from committing murder, Gunn dispatches the professor himself, an act for which Fred cannot forgive him.

What follows is a painful disintegration of their relationship. Fred can no longer bear Gunn to touch her and rebuffs all his attempts at reconciliation ('Apocalypse Nowish').

Fred and Wesley

Wesley clearly has feelings for Fred, but his natural shyness gets in the way of any developing relationship. When he finally plucks up the courage to profess his love to Fred, he is unaware that Gunn has similar ideas and, heartbreakingly, is forced to watch as Fred and Gunn embark on a romantic relationship ('Waiting in the Wings').

Wesley's unrequited love for Fred subsequently has a further hurdle to face in the form of her Wolfram & Hart assistant, Knox, whose infatuation with Fred will ultimately have tragic consequences ('Conviction').

Wesley's feelings for Fred grow stronger and are evident to all but the seemingly oblivious Fred. When the pair are under the influence of a Lorne-induced drunkenness spell, it seems that Wesley will finally seize the moment, but sadly Fred ruins the mood by babbling on about Knox ('Life of the Party').

Another telling moment is Wesley's shooting of a cyborg that he believes to be his father. His explanation that his apparent patricide was prompted not in fear of his own life or in protection of Angel but because the fake Roger Wyndam-Pryce threatened Fred should have been enough to give Fred a clue as to the depth of his feelings. But, still, their relationship remains firmly stuck in a dreadfully inconsequential 'just good friends' mode ('Lineage').

When Wesley and Fred finally start a relationship, at Fred's urging, Gunn gives Wesley his blessing. Adding that if Wesley ever hurts Fred, Gunn will kill him like a chicken.

However, it is an unwitting Gunn who expedites the arrival of a sarcophagus that will cause Fred's death. A shattered Wesley cradles Fred in his arms as she dies and is replaced by the blue-skinned ancient power Illyria ('A Hole in the World').

A devastated Wesley turns to drink and manic despair, agreeing to help Illyria to find her place in this world simply because she looks like his lost love ('Underneath').

As the apocalypse approaches, Wesley is the only member of the team who has no perfect final day to live. Without Fred, his life has no meaning and he spends his last hours comforting and tending to the wounded Illyria. Later, Illyria returns the favour, becoming the image of his beloved Fred and bidding a tender farewell to the dying Wesley, granting him one last moment of happiness in a world that has no place for either of them ('Not Fade Away').

Angel and Nina

Angel fails to prevent Nina from becoming a werewolf ('Unleashed'). However, he attempts to help her to deal with her problem and, in the process, gains a beautiful if occasionally hirsute girlfriend ('Smile Time'). Much to the amusement of his son Connor ('Origin').

'IF YOU'VE GOTTA GO ...'

20 outrageously inventive deaths of characters in *Angel*

 Russell Winters: launched through a plate-glass window with inflammatory results ('City Of').

 Dennis Pearson: walled-up in a chimney breast by his insanely jealous mother ('Rm W/a Vu').

 Marcus: impaled on a particularly dangerous section of Santa Monica's Paradise Cove Pier ('In the Dark').

 Doyle: heroically vaporised in the act of destroying The Scourge's half-breed-extermination-device ('Hero').

 Penn: fatally attached to his Sire with a large piece of two-by-four wielded by, the apparently hyper-strong, Kate Lockley ('Somnambulist').

 Thesulac demon: electrocuted by having its tentacles plugged into the mains. Ouch ('Are You Now, or Have You Ever Been?').

 Holland Manners: locked in his own wine cellar with his guests and two very hungry vampires ('Reunion').

Gio: head bitten off by an outraged demon in a karaoke bar ('That Old Gang of Mine').

 Darla: self-staked as a bizarre-but-courageous alternative to a Caesarean section ('Lullaby').

 Phillip J Spivey: desiccated by translucent supernatural parasitic slug demons ('The Price').

 Daniel Holtz: murdered by his co-conspirator Justine with an ice pick to simulate a vampire attack ('Benediction').

 Professor Seidel: neck broken and thrown into an interdimensional portal ('Supersymmetry').

 Manjet: messily ripped apart by The Beast's master, despite being in a locked and heavily guarded panic-room ('Long Day's Journey').

 The Beast: fatally stabbed with a knife cunningly fashioned from its own body parts ('Salvage').

 Lilah Morgan: throat cut by a possessed Cordelia, then decapitated by erstwhile lover Wesley ('Calvary').

 Magnus Hainsley: decapitated by a well-directed tea tray ('Just Rewards').

 Artode: murdered on the toilet by Lorne's Hulk-like alter ego ('Life of the Party').

Winifred Burkle: infected and hollowed by an ancient being that then takes possession of her empty shell ('A Hole in the World').

 Archduke Sebassis: murdered in his own bathtub by unwittingly drinking the blood of his recently poisoned slave ('Not Fade Away').

 Wesley Wyndam-Pryce: fatally stabbed by a magically manipulated knife in a last-ditch throw-down with Cyvus Vail ('Not Fade Away').

SATURDAY NIGHT AT THE MOVIES ... II

More famous – and infamous – films referenced in *Angel*

- *Roadhouse* ('Couplet').

- *Apocalypse Now* ('Couplet', 'Apocalypse Nowish', 'Lineage', 'Why We Fight').

- *Almost Famous* ('Couplet', 'Sleep Tight', 'Sacrifice', 'Life of the Party').

- *Mr Mom* ('Loyalty').

- *The Great Rock and Roll Swindle* ('Sleep Tight').

- *The Man Who Fell to Earth* ('Forgiving').

- *Bedazzled* ('Double or Nothing').

- *Robin and the Seven Hoods* ('Double or Nothing').

- *Ocean's 11* ('Double or Nothing').

- *The Godfather* ('Double or Nothing', 'Slouching Towards Bethlehem', 'Salvage', 'Conviction', 'Why We Fight', 'The Girl in Question', 'Not Fade Away').

- *Love Story* ('Double or Nothing').

- *Never on Sunday* ('The Price').

- *Jurassic Park* ('The Price').

- *I Know My First Name is Steven* ('A New World').

- *Wild Wild West* ('Benediction').

- *That Thing You Do!* ('Benediction').

- *That Sinking Feeling* ('Tomorrow').

- *Alice Doesn't Live Here Anymore* ('Tomorrow', 'Power Play').

- *Ferris Bueller's Day Off* ('Deep Down').

- *Life Is Beautiful* ('Deep Down').

- *The Graduate* ('Ground State').

- *All Quiet on the Western Front* ('Ground State').

- *Austin Powers: International Man of Mystery* ('Ground State').

- *Diamonds Are Forever* ('The House Always Wins').

- *Enter the Dragon* ('Slouching Towards Bethlehem').

- *Jaws* ('Apocalypse Nowish', 'Soul Purpose').

- *The Ten Commandments* ('Apocalypse Nowish').

- *Legend* ('Apocalypse Nowish').

- *An American Werewolf in London* ('Apocalypse Nowish', 'Unleashed').

- *Dead Man Walking* ('Habeas Corpses').

- *Crouching Tiger, Hidden Dragon* ('Awakening').

- *The Bone Collector* ('Calvary').

- *That's the Way It Is* ('Salvage').
- *The Hunting Party* ('Salvage').
- *Speed* ('Salvage').
- *Beastmaster* ('Release').
- *Picnic at Hanging Rock* ('Players').
- *Clash of the Titans* ('Players').
- *A Clockwork Orange* ('Players').
- *Yellow Submarine* ('Shiny Happy People', 'Power Play').
- *The Greatest Story Ever Told* ('The Magic Bullet').
- *Quest for Fire* ('The Magic Bullet').
- *Captain Clegg* ('Sacrifice').
- *Sunset Boulevard* ('Peace Out').
- *Galaxy Quest* ('Peace Out').
- *The Sorrow and the Pity* ('Conviction').
- *Apollo 13* ('Conviction', 'Why We Fight').
- *JFK* ('Conviction').
- *Towering Inferno* ('Conviction').
- *Monty Python's The Meaning of Life* ('Conviction').
- *Pirates of the Caribbean: The Curse of the Black Pearl* ('Just Rewards').
- *Road Trip* ('Just Rewards').
- *Legal Eagles* ('Life of the Party').
- *A Bridge Too Far* ('Life of the Party').

- *The Music Man* ('Life of the Party', 'Destiny').
- *The Good, the Bad and the Ugly* ('Life of the Party').
- *The Godfather, Part II* ('Life of the Party').
- *El Cid* ('The Cautionary Tale of Numero Cinco').
- *Iron Eagle II* ('Lineage').
- *Robocop* ('Lineage').
- *You've Got Mail* ('Destiny').
- *Chitty Chitty Bang Bang* ('Destiny').
- *His Girl Friday* ('Destiny').
- *Looking for Mr Goodbar* ('Destiny').
- *One Flew Over the Cuckoo's Nest* ('Damage').
- *X-Men* ('Damage').
- *Mean Streets* ('Damage').
- *Urban Cowboy* ('You're Welcome').
- *Charley* ('Smile Time').
- *Anywhere But Here* ('A Hole in the World').
- *The Lord of the Rings* trilogy ('Damage', 'A Hole in the World', 'Power Play').
- *The Addams Family* ('Shells').
- *The Truman Show* ('Underneath').
- *The 'burbs* ('Underneath').
- *Groundhog Day* ('Underneath').
- *Two Days in the Valley* ('Underneath').

- *The Poseidon Adventure* ('Time Bomb').
- *The Last of Sheila* ('Time Bomb').
- *Vertigo* ('Time Bomb').
- *Highlander* ('The Girl in Question').
- *Bring Me the Head of Alfredo Garcia* ('The Girl in Question').
- *Showboat* ('Power Play').
- *The Devil's Advocate* ('Not Fade Away').

HISTORY REPEATING

A definitive guide to *Angel*'s flashback sequences

Angel is the tale of a 242-year-old vampire with a rich and varied history of manic ultraviolence, bloody carnage and, ultimately, a bit of redemption. Tantalising glimpses of the past are presented in a series of flashbacks and we are, thus, able to piece together some fascinating insights into the life and times of Angel/Angelus.

'Somnambulist'
Angel's dreams seem to be coming true. However, investigations prove that there is another vampire in town – Penn, whom Angel sired in the late eighteenth century and who sees Angel as a father who tutored him in the ways of murder.

'The Prodigal'
1753: as a human, Liam was a drunken whoring wastrel who lived down to his father's every expectation. As a vampire, the young and raw Angelus lost little time in taking his revenge through patricide. However, his triumph is short-lived as Darla reminds him that he can now never gain what Liam so desperately wanted, his father's approval. His victory took mere moments, but his father's ultimate defeat of him will last a lifetime.

'Are You Now or Have You Ever Been?'

1952: a reclusive Angel is living at the Hyperion Hotel, where a Thesulac demon is busy spreading fear and driving the residents to suicide and paranoia. Angel tries to help a girl on the run from the police but finds himself on the wrong end of a lynch mob. Disgusted, he abandons the hotel and its residents to their fate.

'Darla'

We see Darla being sired by the Master in Virginia in 1609; Darla introducing Angel to the Master in London in 1760; Drusilla deciding that she wants a playmate in London in 1880; Darla killing the gypsy who cursed Angel in 1898 and then Angel rejoining Darla, Drusilla and Spike in China in 1900.

An absolute masterpiece which forms – with its *Buffy* counterpart, 'Fool for Love' – a movie-length epic with staggering scope (almost 400 years) and themes of lust, passion, sacrifice and, magnificently, redemption. That shot of Angelus, Darla, Drusilla and Spike striding amidst the chaos of the Boxer Rebellion as if they owned the world is a piece of television history.

'Heartthrob'

Angel Investigations liquidates a group of vampires one of whom, Elizabeth, was the eternal love of James, an ex protégé of Angelus. Elizabeth and James travelled with Angelus and Darla circa 1767 at the time when they were being hunted across the capital cities of Europe by Daniel Holtz.

James and Elizabeth were, in many ways, a prototype Spike and Drusilla and when their passionate relationship of 234 years is brought to a dusty end by Angel, James swears revenge, sacrificing his immortality for one day of magical invincibility.

'Lullaby'

York, 1764: in which we learn how Angelus and Darla attacked Holtz's house and murdered his wife and baby son, cruelly allowing Holtz's daughter, Sarah, to be reborn as a vampire. Holtz sings his daughter one last lullaby before forcing her into the morning sun. No wonder the poor man makes a bargain with the demon Sahjhan to gain his ultimate vengeance.

'Soulless'

1789: The Beast attempts to recruit Angelus to kill a trio of women called the Svear Priestesses who possess the power to remove The Beast from this dimension.

'Orpheus'

Spiked by Faith's drug-tainted blood, Angelus spirals back into the private hell of Angel's history, including his arrival in America in 1902, rescuing of a puppy in Chicago in 1920 and his 1970s lapse – feeding from a dying doughnut-shop clerk, which subsequently led to over two decades of guilt and despair.

'Destiny'

1880: Angelus and William are formally introduced by Drusilla at the Royal London Hotel. Angelus is delighted

143

to have a male companion and sets about teaching William the ways of the vampire world, which include a massacre at a wedding during which Angelus horribly murders a priest and beats the groom to death with his own arm before abducting the bride. William is, initially, impressed but soon finds out that Angelus wishes to share more than the kill when he discovers his mentor bedding his beloved Drusilla.

'Damage'
A deranged Slayer relives both her own past and the pasts of two dead Slayers, with devastating consequences for Spike, whom she mistakes for the vampire who murdered her family.

'Why We Fight'
1943: Angel is persuaded to join the US war effort as one of Uncle Sam's secret weapons against the Nazis when a captured U-boat goes missing in hostile waters.

On board are three of the nastiest vampires in history including, inevitably, Spike, who was lured into a trap by the promise of a 'free virgin blood party'. After completing the mission and having given Spike his freedom and sired Lawson (who will return 60 years hence to cause trouble), Angel swam ashore in Maine and went AWOL.

'The Girl in Question'
Handsome, suave and – seemingly – a stallion between the sheets, The Immortal is, according to Spike, the foulest evil that Hell ever vomited forth. He had Angelus and Spike detained in Rome in 1894 so that he could have his wicked

way with Darla and Drusilla (simultaneously). Much to *their* delight and Angelus and Spike's impotent fury.

There is also a brief, but interesting, glimpse of Spike and Dru in a monochrome beatnik Fellini-style 50s Italy. *Ciao*.

'GIVE US FAITH, LORD,' THEY CRIED. AND, LO, FAITH WAS GIVEN UNTO THEM

What happens when good Slayers go bad ... then good again

A native of South Boston, Faith had an unhappy childhood with, it would seem, an absentee father and an alcoholic mother.

 When meeting the Scooby Gang for the first time, she bemoans that her life could have been very different if she'd had a gang of friends around her. Instead, she drifted through her teens with a series of very unpleasant-sounding boyfriends, including one who liked to dress her up in a schoolgirl uniform and indulge in S&M games. Her life only achieved any meaning in 1998 when, after the death of Kendra in Sunnydale, Faith was chosen as the next Slayer.

 Quickly found by her (female) Watcher, Faith threw herself, eagerly, into the Slayer lifestyle – her wild and undisciplined attitude towards killing being tempered by a natural affinity with combat. However, when the ancient vampire Kakistos killed her Watcher, Faith fled to Sunnydale to seek help from her Slayer-predecessor, Buffy.

Despite the pair defeating Kakistos, and subsequent attacks, it was clear that Faith never truly fitted in with the Scooby Gang – feeling herself to be an outsider in their organised and structured world. The cracks first began to show when The Council seemingly sent Faith a new Watcher, Gwendolyn Post. Ms Post, in fact, turned out to be a rogue Watcher, which further disillusioned an already unstable Faith.

Having led Buffy down some dark and troubling alleyways, Faith committed the ultimate Slayer crime, killing a human – the Mayor's assistant Allen Finch. Due to a mixture of psychosis and denial, she attempted to lay the blame for this on Buffy but, fortunately, Rupert Giles was wise enough to see through Faith's web of lies.

Angel, himself no stranger to the complicated and difficult nature of redemption, believed that he could save Faith and set her on the right road, but the unfortunate intervention of Faith's new Watcher, Wesley Wyndam-Pryce, ended any hope of Faith's rehabilitation and Faith found herself a new position as the right-hand assassin of Sunnydale's Mayor, Richard Wilkins, with whom, for the first time in her life, she felt wanted and appreciated.

With the Mayor, Faith was able to kill anyone she wanted and had a great time messing with the schemes of Buffy and her friends until, finally, the two Slayers confronted each other and Buffy stabbed Faith with her own knife and then threw her from a rooftop just hours before the apocalyptic events of Graduation Day.

Faith then spent eight months in a coma while Sunnydale changed around her. Awakening, confused and alone, she was left one final gift by Wilkins, a device that allowed her to swap bodies with Buffy and, briefly, assume her nemesis's identity.

However, elements of Buffy's life clearly struck a chord with Faith and, after helping to save a church full of worshippers from vampires, Faith found herself in the uncomfortable position of confronting her neuroses by, literally, beating herself up before Buffy was able – with Willow and Tara's help – to effect a reversal spell.

So, Faith headed for Los Angeles, and into the eager arms of Wolfram & Hart. Hired by the sinister law firm to assassinate Angel, Faith's agenda was, actually, much cleverer than that. She kidnapped her former Watcher, Wesley, and subjected him to unbelievable torture purely – it would seem – to get Angel interested in her enough to kill her and end her miserable existence ('Five by Five').

Angel, of course, had other – more redemptive – ideas in mind. Despite pressure from Cordy, Wesley, an elite Council wetworks squad and, subsequently, Buffy herself, Angel determined to give Faith the chance that he, himself, had been given, to put right the sins of the past; although he does tell her that even if she spends the rest of her life helping people it may, still, never cancel out the suffering she has caused ('Sanctuary'). Faith elects to pay for her crimes and Angel subsequently visits her in prison where she is quietly serving her time and coming to terms with the rage inside her ('Judgment').

Two years later, however, when Angel's soul disappears, Wesley realises that the help of a Slayer will be needed to recover it and stages a jailbreak ('Salvage'). A grateful Faith then sets about helping Wes, Gunn, Connor and Fred in tracking down Angelus and is able to destroy The Beast and, thus, unblock the sun above Los Angeles ('Release').

 Faith realises that the only way to get Angelus's soul back is to get inside him and so allows her own, drug-tainted, blood to be drunk. While her body lies apparently at death's door, Faith enters Angel's mind and accompanies Angelus on a hallucinogenic trip through the last hundred years of the vampire's existence ('Orpheus').

 When Willow casts the spell that restores Angel's soul, Faith is strong enough to leave his mind and, thanks to her Slayer strength, recover from her ordeal. She leaves LA with the gratitude of Angel and his friends, and it seems that Faith's rehabilitation is almost complete.

 Returning to Sunnydale with Willow, Faith – despite a few awkward moments – is on hand to help Buffy, Spike and the potential Slayers defeat the armies of Hell and the First Evil, and close the Hellmouth for good. Along the way, she makes a new friend – the handsome Robin Wood. She survives the final battle along with most of the Scooby Gang and, although her future is uncertain, her place within the newly re-established Council of Watchers is assured should she want it.

 The authors. however, prefer to imagine Faith riding from city to city across the US on a motorbike searching, perhaps for the rest of her life, for further redemption and for evil to fight.

149

WE HARDLY KNEW YE, BUT WE KILLED YE ANYWAY

Further outrageously inventive deaths of extras in *Angel*

 Bug demon: flattened by a bus driven by an extremely pissed-off parent ('Fredless').

 Various vampires and demons: blown to smithereens by an exploding fake baby ('Dad').

 Butler: stabbed between the eyes with a lethal teaspoon ('Just Rewards').

 Wolfram & Hart lawyer: sliced and diced with enough goo left over to fill two buckets ('Just Rewards').

 Assorted acolytes: ingested by a people-eating Power That Was in the furtherance of love, peace and happiness ('Shiny Happy People', 'Peace Out').

 Security guard in ice factory: incinerated by an overheated Oden-Tal ('She').

Thugs: crushed by a telekinetically powered dumpster ('Untouched').

 Man in hotel room: driven to suicide by a whispering paranoia demon ('Are You Now, or Have You Ever Been'?).

 Demon: beheaded by Fred's cunning toaster/decapitation device ('Fredless').

 Fez-wearing psychic: brain-speared by a metal bar ('That Vision Thing').

 Policewoman: beaten to death by a male colleague possessed by murderous misogynistic rage ('Billy').

 Werewolf: killed with an inscribed silver pen ('Unleashed').

 The entire staff of Wolfram & Hart: slaughtered by The Beast then zombified by their employers ('Habeas Corpses').

'STOP CALLING ME PASTRIES'

12 classic lines of dialogue from *Angel*'s Season 3

 Angel: 'That's Merl.' Gunn: 'Where's the rest of him?' Angel: 'I stopped by this morning, thought I'd give "sincere" one more shot. Even brought doughnuts … So far, we've ruled out suicide.' ('That Old Gang of Mine')

 Angel: 'I'm *not* a eunuch.' Cordelia: 'Just a figure of speech.' Angel: 'Find a *better* one.' ('Carpe Noctem')

 Cordelia, to Billy: 'I'm feeling superior because I have an arrow pointed at your jugular. And the irony of using a phallic-shaped weapon is *not* lost on me.' ('Billy')

 Holtz: 'You said you work for the law.' Lilah: 'No, I said I'm a lawyer. I don't *care* about the law.' ('Lullaby')

 Lorne: 'Is that bacon I smell or did somebody fall asleep with the curtains open?' ('Dad')

 Cordy: '*You've* seen *The Matrix*?' Skip: 'Loved that flick! When Trinity's all "Dodge this!" … I'm not really instilling awe anymore, am I?' ('Birthday')

152

Fred: 'We're watching the exact same troupe you saw in 1990?' Gunn: 'I think he said *1890*.' Fred: 'OK, that's *much more* impossible.' ('Waiting in the Wings')

 The Loa: 'Your insolence is displeasing.' Wesley: '*You* try chatting with a cranky hamburger.' ('Loyalty')

 Wesley: 'You're a soldier. You work for a man who you think is noble and good. I respect that. Trouble is, he's not.' Justine: 'You work with a vampire.' Wesley: 'Who, in fact, *is* noble and good. Quirky, but there it is.' ('Sleep Tight')

 Angel: 'You look like hell. Not the fun one where they burn you with hot pokers for all eternity, but the hardcore one. You know, Nixon and Britney Spears?' ('Sleep Tight')

 Gunn: 'Folks not used to seeing a kid in animal skins riding on top of a bus. Well, not south of Santa Monica Boulevard, anyway.' ('A New World')

 Connor: 'Filthy demon.' Lorne: 'Actually, that's *Uncle* Filthy Demon to you.' ('Benediction')

CANCEL MY SUBSCRIPTION TO THE RESURRECTION

15 Los Angeles inhabitants who make the greatest comeback since Lazarus

Although many characters in *Angel* meet untimely (and sticky) ends, some have an awkward tendency to refuse to actually *remain* dead for very long. The options are many and varied – vampires, ghosts, non-corporeal entities, zombies, mystical resurrections and eternal contracts with evil law firms. In Los Angeles, death genuinely isn't an end in and of itself, but rather a new beginning.

Sharon Richler, Kevin, Neil and a nameless bartender
All get a nasty death, a brief resurrection and a spectacularly messy ending, as a parasitic body-swapping entity stalks the singles bars of LA ('Lonely Heart').

Dennis and Maud Pearson
This pair may be deceased, but their ghostly presence is still very much in evidence, although mommy dearest is swiftly sent to her eternal punishment by her son (whom she walled up alive many years ago). Phantom Dennis stays put, however, as a helpful, if somewhat possessive, flatmate for Cordelia ('Rm W/a Vu').

Darla

A woman of independent means, sired in 1609 by The Master and resurrected as a vampire ('Darla').

Many years later she would be destroyed by Angel ('Angel'), only to be resurrected as a human through the machinations of Wolfram & Hart ('To Shanshu in LA'). However, Darla's regained humanity also includes the terminal syphilis she was dying from in colonial Virginia and, having failed to win her a mystical reprieve, Angel prepares to help her to face death with dignity.

Tragically, he is overpowered by Wolfram & Hart's minions and forced to watch as Drusilla sires Darla to vampire status once more ('The Trial').

Finally, impossibly pregnant with Angel's child, Darla kills herself, driving a stake through her own heart to allow her baby, Connor, to be born ('Lullaby').

After a record-breaking four deaths, you'd think that Darla would be glad of a rest but she makes one final appearance as a ghostly apparition trying to convince Connor not to commit murder ('Inside Out').

Zombie cops

Peter Harkes (1965–2000) and Kevin Helenbrook (1967–2000), resurrected to bring peace and order to the streets of LA. By any means necessary, including extreme racial prejudice and manic ultraviolence ('The Thin Dead Line').

Holland Manners

Killed by hungry vampires in his own wine cellar ('Reunion') but still very much part of the Wolfram & Hart empire. Holland explains to a surprised Angel that he is, indeed, quite dead; it's just that his contract extends well beyond that ('Reprise').

Harmony Kendall

When Harmony pays a visit to her old friend Cordelia, the two have much to talk about. Many things have changed since their last meeting in Sunnydale. Cordelia is now an office manager, while Harmony is ... dead. Actually, Cordelia is quite relieved to discover that Harmony is a vampire – for a while, she thought her old friend was gay ('Disharmony').

Billy Blim

Dead and confined to a deserved fiery hell until Angel reluctantly rescues him, once resurrected the demonic Blim wreaks havoc – unleashing misogynistic rage in every male he touches. Ultimately, Blim is killed for the second, and hopefully final, time by a bruised but defiant Lilah Morgan ('Billy').

The staff of Wolfram & Hart

Killed by the rampaging Beast and then resurrected as zombies to protect the ruined building against intruders ('Habeas Corpses'). More zombies continue to patrol the subterranean vaults ('You're Welcome').

Lilah Morgan

Having been just about the only member of Wolfram & Hart to escape the zombification, Lilah is subsequently stabbed by a possessed Cordelia ('Calvary'). She then suffers the indignity of beheading by a grieving Wesley ('Salvage'). However, as Holland Manners previously noted, a contract with Wolfram & Hart is, quite literally, eternal and Lilah returns to tempt the Angel Investigations team with the resources of the firm ('Home').

Spike
Heroically immolated in a pillar of redemptive fire in Sunnydale, Spike is less than delighted to be disgorged from an amulet in Los Angeles some weeks later, alive, but in a frustratingly incorporeal state ('Conviction').

Matthias Pavayne
An eighteenth-century surgeon with a fatal line in treatment. Sacrificed by Wolfram & Hart to consecrate the site of their Los Angeles branch, Pavayne continues to provide a useful service as a psychic clean-up operative, luring the spirits of deceased employees into Hell to take his own place ('Hellbound').

Cordelia Chase
Apparently awakened from a coma to help Angel regain his mission, all is not as it seems. Cordelia is, it would seem, already dead and her intervention was a favour from The Powers That Be for services rendered. Cordy leaves Angel with one last kiss and vanishes as he receives the tragic news of her death ('You're Welcome').

Ensign Sam Lawson
Part of a volunteer force that captured a U-boat for US military intelligence in 1943. Sadly the cargo – some of the nastiest vampires in Europe – escaped and started killing

the crew. Angel, given the mission of saving the boat, befriended Lawson but, when Lawson was stabbed by a German prisoner, Angel was forced to make the young submariner into a vampire in order to get the U-boat's engines running again.

Angel then set the newly undead Lawson free. Sadly, Lawson wandered unhappily through the next 60 years, never fully comfortable with his life as a vampire and, finally, he tracks Angel down, seeking revenge. This time, when Angel kills him, he stays dead ('Why We Fight').

Illyria
An ancient being, entombed within the Deeper Well and released from her sarcophagus by a curious Winifred Burkle ('A Hole in the World'). Illyria is resurrected in the shell of Fred's body ('Shells').

Lindsey McDonald
Relegated to a hell-like holding dimension by Wolfram & Hart, where he has his heart ripped out on a daily basis, Lindsey is rescued by Gunn, who selflessly takes McDonald's place for two weeks of torture before being rescued by Illyria ('Underneath'). Subsequently, a surprised Lindsey is executed by Lorne. He always believed that his nemesis, Angel, would be the one to end his existence ('Not Fade Away').

RUMOURS OF MY DEATH HAVE BEEN
GREATLY EXAGGERATED

LA inhabitants who seemed to die but, actually, didn't

Francis Doyle
Seemingly killed by Angel. Having one's head rotated through 180 degrees would finish off most people – luckily, Brachen demons can't be dispatched that easily. Sadly, the reprieve is only temporary ('Hero').

Angel
Apparently hanged by an enraged lynch mob in 1952. However, vampires don't actually need their windpipe and, as soon as they're gone, Angel quietly slips out of the noose ('Are You Now or Have You Ever Been?').

Lorne
Had his head removed and served on a platter to an anguished Princess Cordelia. However, as with all of the Deathwok Clan, since his body remained un-mutilated he lived to sing another day ('Through the Looking Glass', 'There's No Place Like Plrtz Glrb').

Daniel Holtz
Not actually dead, but frozen in time for 227 years, planning his revenge on Angel. A revenge which, when he is

reawakened in the twenty-first century ('Quickening'), he takes with brutal effectiveness ('Sleep Tight').

The Blinnikov Ballet Company
Pulled out of reality by the evil Count Kurskov and forced to dance the same production of *Giselle* for eternity until Angel and Cordelia help the doomed ballerina to change the dance, break the spell and, presumably, die ('Waiting in the Wings').

Charles Gunn
Had his heart stopped by the electrifying cat burglar Gwen Raiden who, luckily, was also able to reverse the problem ('Ground State').

Voynok demon
Having had its head ripped off by Angel, this tricky customer simply grows another one. It seems that not only can the Voynok demon regenerate body parts but, like a cat, it has a rather handy nine lives ('Supersymmetry').

Roger Wyndam-Pryce
Despite apparently being killed by his son Wesley, in defence of Fred, the real Mr Wyndam-Pryce senior is very much alive and kicking back in England. Wesley's seeming patricide was the result of the substitution of a cunningly disguised cyborg ('Lineage').

LOGIC, LET ME INTRODUCE YOU TO THIS WINDOW

Things in *Angel* that make absolutely no logical sense

It's *inevitable* that, even in the most inventive and intelligent of series, there are going to be a few goofs, plot-holes, logic mistakes and continuity errors. Part of the fun of being a fan is looking for these and pointing them out, loudly, on the Internet. Then, when any non-fans point out the same things, hitting them, hard, on top of the head with this book. Here are some of the more thought-provoking screw-ups in *Angel*.

As with various *Buffy* episodes, Angel can be seen on film and videotape, despite all cameras using mirrors as part of their focusing mechanism (see 'City Of', 'Somnambulist', 'Sanctuary', 'Are You Now or Have You Ever Been?' and many others). If a vampire can have his picture taken, why is Angel so fascinated with his reflection in 'I Will Remember You' and 'Through the Looking Glass'?

In 'City Of', Doyle uses the fact that he walked uninvited into Angel's home as proof that Doyle is not a vampire. But it's later established that a vampire's home is not protected from other vampires entering, since the owner is dead.

161

(This also explains how Angel can get into both Tina's apartment after she's been killed and Russell's mansion. Russell's ability to enter Tina's apartment is specifically explained by the fact that he owns the building.)

However, considering all of the above, why does Angel need an invitation to enter Fred's room in 'Heartthrob'? The Hyperion is a hotel – more specifically, it's *Angel's* hotel – so, surely all the rooms are either public domain or, even if they aren't, they belong to him. Perhaps he's simply being a gentleman?

In 'Rm W/a Vu' we discover that vampires can, it would seem, be invited into a home even if they are nowhere near the home at the time (and, in this case, when it hasn't been rented yet).

Angel drinks coffee in 'I Fall to Pieces' (and several subsequent episodes), despite the fact that in *Buffy*: 'The Prom' he told Joyce Summers he didn't because it makes him jittery.

Kate tells Angel that she's read about his past, in 'Somnambulist'. In *Buffy*: 'Angel', Giles said that he could find no mention of Angelus in the texts, but he did discover references in *The Watcher's Diaries*. Kate's line, 'a demon with the face of an angel,' is exactly what Giles reads in the former episode. With The Watcher's Council's desire for secrecy it seems remiss that they've let this highly secretive publication into the public domain.

In 'I've Got You Under My Skin', Angel tells Paige, 'I'm not a big bleeder'. He shouldn't, actually, be a bleeder *at all*, as his heart doesn't beat. But he is seen to bleed in numerous episodes.

There is a huge discontinuity between 'Eternity' and the *Buffy* episodes 'Surprise' and 'Innocence'. It's established in the latter that one moment of perfect happiness will turn Angel into Angelus even if he doesn't feel much happiness after the transformation. Yet in 'Eternity' it is implied (and subsequently confirmed) that he will only remain Angelus as long as he is experiencing the effects of the drug. Once he comes down, he reverts to Angel. If that's the case, why did it take eight episodes and a *spell* to revert him in *Buffy* Season 2?

 The exterior shot of Faith's jail in 'Judgment' is Folsom Prison – the one Johnny Cash so memorably sang about. But, isn't that an all-male establishment?

 It's implied in 'Reunion' that vampires first rise between sundown on the day they died and dawn the next day, which flatly contradicts several *Buffy* episodes ('Welcome to the Hellmouth', 'Helpless' and 'The Freshman') and, indeed, several subsequent *Angel* stories ('Why We Kill', for example).

 When Gunn first went to Caritas in 'Guise Will Be Guise' he wondered how he'd lived in LA all his life and not noticed such weird-ass stuff going on? Yet he was, seemingly, aware of a demon Casino from an early age ('Double or Nothing').

 Sirk notes in 'Destiny' that the Cup of Perpetual Torment was first housed in the hidden city of Petra. It disappeared during the Crusades and resurfaced in the Vatican only to vanish once more during the third year of the Inquisition. (As this began in 1232, that would place the cup's disappearance in or around 1235.)

From there it, somehow, found it's way to Nevada. Thus, once again, we have an example of a mythical artefact from the ancient world in the *Buffy*-universe being hidden on a continent unknown to all the world – except the indigenous population and, allegedly, a few lost Vikings – until 1492 (see also *Buffy*: 'The Harsh Light of Day' and 'End of Days'). Who took the cup there? How did they know that they wouldn't fall off the end of the world?

We see Angel driving quite often and it's reasonable that sometime within the last 100 years he would have learned the basics. However, assuming that his car is within the specifications of California State law, and given that he's had a *certain* amount of contact with the police, if he were ever asked to produce a valid driving licence, could he? Driving tests are normally conducted during the day, with all that pesky sunlight about.

'TELEVISION, THE DRUG OF THE NATION'

TV shows referenced or alluded to in *Angel*

- *Mission: Impossible* ('Lonely Heart', 'Blind Date').
- *The Naked City* ('Lonely Heart').
- *The Flintstones* ('In the Dark').
- *I Love Lucy* ('In the Dark').
- *Late Night with Conan O'Brien* ('Sense and Sensitivity').
- *Gentle Ben* ('Sense and Sensitivity').
- *Star Trek* ('Sense and Sensitivity', 'Happy Anniversary', 'Belonging', 'Over the Rainbow', 'Damage', 'Time Bomb').
- *Forever Knight* ('I Will Remember You', 'Somnambulist', 'Are You Now or Have You Ever Been?' 'Darla').
- *Roots* ('Hero').
- *Seinfeld* ('Hero').
- *Police Woman* ('Somnambulist').
- *The Dating Game* ('Expecting').
- *Jeopardy* ('The Ring').
- *Wheel of Fortune* ('The Ring', 'Belonging').

- *The Jerry Springer Show* ('The Ring').

- *The X-Files* ('Sanctuary', 'Happy Anniversary', 'That Vision Thing', 'Apocalypse Nowish').

- *Blackadder* ('Are You Now or Have You Ever Been?' 'The Magic Bullet', 'Life of the Party', 'Shells').

- *The Incredible Hulk* ('Untouched').

- *Charmed* ('Untouched').

- *Friends* ('The Shroud of Rahmon', 'Birthday').

- *Survivor* ('The Trial').

- *The Prisoner* ('The Trial').

- *The Jeffersons* ('The Thin Dead Line').

- *Sesame Street* ('Disharmony', 'Smile Time').

- *The Jetsons* ('Dead End').

- *Happy Days* ('Over the Rainbow').

- *Mr Roger's Neighborhood* ('Over the Rainbow').

- *Xena: Warrior Princess* ('Over the Rainbow').

- *Monty Python's Flying Circus* ('Through the Looking Glass', 'Offspring', 'Provider', 'Destiny').

- *Kolchak: The Night Stalker* ('Carpe Noctem', 'Awakening').

- *Judge Judy* ('Fredless').

- *Gunsmoke* ('Quickening').

- *The Mary Tyler Moore Show* ('Birthday').

- *Doctor Who* ('Provider', 'Inside Out', 'Lineage').

- *Candid Camera* ('Loyalty').

- *The Flying Nun* ('Sleep Tight').
- *Twin Peaks* ('Forgiving').
- *Star Trek: Deep Space Nine* ('Forgiving').
- *Roswell* ('Forgiving').
- *The West Wing* ('The Price', 'Damage').
- *The Simpsons* ('Spin the Bottle', 'Salvage', 'The Girl in Question').
- *Voyage to the Bottom of the Sea* ('Long Day's Journey').
- *Dark Shadows* ('Release').
- *The Brady Bunch* ('Release').
- *Stargate SG-1* ('Release').
- *Futurama* ('Release').
- *Scooby Doo, Where Are You?* ('Release').
- *Bonanza* ('Inside Out').
- *Star Trek: The Next Generation* ('Sacrifice').
- *The Twilight Zone* ('Peace Out').
- *I, Claudius* ('Peace Out').
- *MacGyver* ('Home').
- *Joanie Loves Chachi* ('Conviction').
- *Captain Kangaroo* ('Just Rewards').
- *The Littlest Hobo* ('Just Rewards').
- *Land of the Lost* ('Hellbound').
- *Top Cat* ('Life of the Party').

- *South Park* ('Life of the Party').
- *The Bionic Woman* ('Lineage').
- *Hong Kong Phooey* ('Destiny').
- *Miami Vice* ('Soul Purpose').
- *One Foot in the Grave* ('You're Welcome').
- *Father Ted* ('Shells').
- Eddie Izzard's *Circle* ('Shells') and *Dress to Kill* ('The Girl in Question').
- *Knight Rider* ('Underneath').
- *Leave it to Beaver* ('Underneath').
- *The Carol Burnett Show* ('Not Fade Away').

EVERY LITTLE BIT HURTS
The confusing life and times of Winifred Burkle

When a disturbance at Caritas leads Angel and his friends to a
strange book and a missing girl, it's the beginning of a new era for
the team.

 Winifred Burkle, a librarian who was studying to be a
physicist, disappeared in May 1996 in the Foreign
Languages Section of the LA Public Library while reading
a book called *SCRSQWRN* ('Belonging'). The team's investigations lead them through a portal into a strange new
world. In the alternate dimension of Pylea, where humans
are treated as cow-slaves, Fred has survived as a fugitive,
despite being close to insanity. However, her attempt to
help Cordelia leads to her own capture ('Over the
Rainbow').

 When Angel is invited to be the honoured guest at a
Backnaal and swing the crebbil he is alarmed to find that
he's expected to sacrifice Fred. Instead, he rescues her. Fred
is, obviously, overjoyed that the handsome man has saved
her from the monsters, although she suspects that either he
isn't real or she is actually dead. Her fears seem justified
when Angel's demon-self manifests. Despite her terror,

169

Fred saves Gunn and Wesley from the Angel-beast before luring it back to her cave ('Through the Looking Glass'). It is Fred's mathematical genius that opens the portal, which gets the team home to Los Angeles where her process of rehabilitation begins ('There's No Place Like Plrtz Glrb').

Fred's first few months in LA are complicated by the absence of Angel who, following the death of Buffy, has gone to a retreat in Sri Lanka. Fred locks herself in her room where she covers the walls with mathematical formulae ('Heartthrob'). Once out of her room, Fred still prefers to sit under tables but makes rapid progress ('That Vision Thing').

Matters are not helped when Fred's first visit to Caritas coincides with a bloodbath. Perhaps appropriately, her choice of karaoke song is Patsy Cline's 'Crazy' ('That Old Gang of Mine'). Further complications arise when Fred's parents arrive at the Hyperion and Fred, apparently terrified, flees.

This is not a case of abuse, however; Fred's parents genuinely love her. She fears that if she reconnects with her old life she will have to acknowledge that the horrors of her banishment to Pylea really happened. Once she accepts this and chooses to remain with her friends at the Hyperion, Fred's healing can begin in earnest ('Fredless').

But, this being LA, the path of reintegration does not run smoothly and Fred has to deal not only with assorted demons, but also with her friends being infected with misogynistic rage and hunting her down. Luckily, her time in Pylea has honed both her survival instincts and her powers of forgiveness ('Billy').

Fred's intellectual abilities make her an asset to the team and her fey feminine personality is also attractive. It's unsurprising that, while Angel merely seems to feel protective towards her, both Gunn and Wesley fall deeply in love with Fred at almost exactly the same time. Fred, meanwhile, seems to be oblivious to this ('Provider'). Ultimately it is Gunn who makes the first move during a (literally enchanted) evening at the ballet ('Waiting in the Wings').

Fred and Gunn subsequently try to balance their work life and their new relationship, while Wesley immerses himself in his work as an escape from the pain of unrequited love ('Couplet'). Fred misguidedly attempts a spot of matchmaking for Wesley with the apparently lonely single mum Aubrey. However, Aubrey is one of Holtz's rabble army and leads Fred and Gunn into a trap from which they are lucky to escape ('Loyalty').

Fred's attempts to reason with a murderous Angel after Wesley's apparent betrayal are unsuccessful ('Forgiving'). Despite Wesley's subsequent banishment from the team she is grateful for her former friend's assistance when Angel's use of dark magic leads to her being infected by parasitic creatures ('The Price').

After Connor returns from Quor-Toth and takes a terrible revenge on his father, an unsuspecting Fred and Gunn shelter and support the teenager while searching for their missing boss and trying to keep the business afloat. However, kind, nurturing Fred shows another side to her character when Connor's duplicity is revealed, savagely attacking him with a taser ('Deep Down').

The less compassionate side to Fred's character can also be seen when the team visit the missing Cordelia's apartment. Fred loses her temper with Phantom Dennis, yelling that Cordelia is not coming back, a response that shows a surprising lack of empathy ('Ground State').

However, Fred's devotion to her duty and to helping the helpless continues to lead her into dark and dangerous territory. It's not every friend who would help you out by painting herself green and donning a skimpy costume, but Fred does this willingly to assist Lorne ('The House Always Wins').

Fred's genius isn't confined to designing the firm's website or interpreting arcane riddles. She also finds time to pursue her scientific research and is thrilled to have a paper on string theory published and to be invited to an elite symposium. However, she narrowly escapes being sucked into another alternate dimension and is enraged to discover that her old teacher, Professor Seidel, has been using portals to get rid of dangerously promising students.

When Angel and Gunn fail to support her in her quest for revenge, Fred approaches Wesley, who helps her devise a plan to send the professor through one of his own portals. Gunn intervenes, murdering Seidel to save Fred from the consequences of her rage. It's an act which Fred cannot forgive and it marks the painful end of their relationship ('Supersymmetry').

Fred's reputation as an innocent ingénue is further tarnished when the team are regressed to their teenage personas and it's revealed that young Winifred had a penchant for smoking weed. It's always the quiet ones, isn't it? ('Spin the Bottle').

When the team are forced to bring Angelus back, the caged vampire taunts Fred with graphic details of what he would like to do to her. His taunts, however, only serve to bring Fred and Wesley closer together ('Soulless'). However, it will be a long time before the couple finally admit the depths of their attraction and the desperate state of LA leaves little time for romance or introspection.

It is Fred who calls Willow to help locate and restore Angel's soul and the two women seem to bond – although Willow misreads the signals and makes it clear that she's currently in a relationship ('Orpheus').

It's not surprising that Fred is giving out mixed signals. Due to her time in Pylea, she can be endearingly dense where human relationships are concerned. She wonders how Connor and Cordy began their liaison. Wesley notes that they were probably lonely. Fred still can't grasp the concept so Wesley uses his own, somewhat sordid, relationship with Lilah Morgan as an example. Relationships, he explains, aren't always about holding hands. Fred remains, frankly, baffled by this revelation ('Players').

Fate decrees that Fred is soon to learn about a loneliness and isolation far worse than that which she suffered in Pylea – the pain of being reviled by your friends.

173

When the messianic Jasmine is incarnated, Fred initially worships her along with everyone else. But, upon coming into contact with Jasmine's blood, she sees Jasmine's true face and becomes a hunted fugitive ('Shiny Happy People'). Fred solves the problem of how to free her friends from Jasmine's thrall and, thus, contributes significantly to the ending of world peace and its replacement with the re-establishment of free will ('Peace Out').

An impressed Wolfram & Hart offer Angel and his friends the chance to take over their LA branch. All of the team, for their own reasons, accept – Fred largely because of the considerable resources that the science department has to offer. It's a decision that will cost Fred dearly ('Home').

Fred seems happy in her state-of-the-art science lab with her personable new assistant Knox as she and her team get straight to work trying to neutralise a viral bomb ('Conviction'). However, Fred is soon distracted by the arrival of an incorporeal Spike, whose existence puzzles her ('Just Rewards'). She quickly finds herself, much to Angel's annoyance, vastly overspending her department's budget and focusing considerable resources on a quest to recorporealise the vampire. Her efforts end in failure but she does succeed in ridding the building of the malevolent spirit of Pavayne and, in the process, wins Spike's undying affection and gratitude ('Hellbound').

Meanwhile, Wesley continues to pine over Fred and she continues to remain impervious to this, seeking instead the company of Knox ('Life of the Party'). The depths of Wesley's affection for Fred are, perhaps, best shown by his rage when Fred is seemingly threatened by his own father ('Lineage').

Fred also attempts to become more sociable, offering herself as confidante for the confused Harmony. For her pains she ends up bound, gagged and thrown in a cupboard ('Harm's Way').

 Tellingly, when Angel falls into a parasite-induced dream state it is Fred who has the most insight into Angel's state of mind. She conducts a bizarre autopsy, revealing that his soul is a dead fish, his heart is a dried up walnut and what remains is a howling abyss ('Soul Purpose').

 Fred's seeming medical expertise is put to more conventional use when she arranges to have Spike's severed arms reattached following an attack by a psychotic Slayer ('Damage').

 Fred finally discovers that Wesley has feelings for her and that these feelings are mutual. She rejects the valentine card from Knox and embarks on a long-delayed relationship with the overjoyed Wesley ('Smile Time').

 Tragically, after all the danger she has faced, it's Fred's scientific curiosity that leads to her downfall. When a mysterious stone sarcophagus arrives in her laboratory she cannot resist a closer look and, unknowingly, she ingests a lethal pathogen. As the team make desperate attempts to save her life, Fred and Wesley spend a final day together. Wesley is then forced to watch as Fred's internal organs liquefy. Fred faces death as bravely as she has faced life, mourning that she will never get to spend time with the man whom she now knows that she loves. Wesley comforts his dying beloved and Fred dies in his arms with one last desperate plea to be allowed to stay ('A Hole in the World').

Her body is hollowed out and occupied by the Old One, Illyria, but Fred is gone forever. All that she was has vanished and her friends can only mourn her loss, avenge her death and try to make peace with the creature who now wears her face and can, by a simple modulation, also adopt her voice and persona with devastatingly painful consequences ('The Girl in Question').

 It's tempting, however, to feel that Fred would have approved of Illyria's final impersonation of her, cradling a dying Wesley and tenderly bidding him farewell. And it's heartbreaking to think that, since Fred's soul was destroyed, these two star-crossed lovers cannot be together even in death ('Not Fade Away').

'I'VE BEEN *FORKING* WITH GUNN'

Classic double entendres in *Angel*

As might be expected from a show that featured what may be television's first recorded use of the euphemism 'stiffener' to describe a beautiful woman ('City Of'), *Angel* included some genuinely saucy *Carry On*-style innuendo.

From Wesley's concealed weapon springing to attention as Fred talks of anal probes ('Spin the Bottle') to Angel assaying the concealing coat and awkward walk of the seriously over-excited ('Waiting in the Wings'), it's enough to make your auntie swoon.

 Cordelia, referring to philanthropist David Nabbit's name, notes that it 'feels good in your mouth' ('War Zone').

 Angel, as the gang prepare to vanquish the Thesulac demon, tells them to watch its tentacles. 'Excuse me?' asks Cordelia. 'Tent-a-cles,' confirms Wesley ('Are You Now or Have You Ever Been?').

 Gunn admires his new home-made axe and hopes that he will get the chance to stick it in something. Men are *all* alike, notes Cordelia ('Untouched').

177

Angel: 'Were you in Virginia?' Wesley: 'That's beside the point' ('Guise Will Be Guise').

When Angel tells Gunn and Wesley that he has had a recent epiphany, Gunn asks if he means that he woke up 'and *bang*'? It was sort of the other way round, replies Angel concerning his liaison with Darla ('Epiphany').

The Transuding Furies suggest that only Angel is equipped to repay the debt that they are owed. Cordelia, after a brief pause, realises exactly what they're talking about ('That Old Gang of Mine').

Groosalugg says that Gunn is very fortunate to have a woman such as Fred looking after his weapon. 'I'm not touching that one,' adds Lorne quickly ('Double or Nothing').

Gunn notes that being close to Gwen can really screw up your equipment ('Inside Out').

Angel tells Lindsey that he wants him, then adds that he's thinking of rephrasing that sentiment. Lindsey replies that he would be much more comfortable if Angel could do just that ('Not Fade Away').

HAUNTED HOTEL CALIFORNIA

Everything you never knew about Angel Investigations'
second base of operations, but were afraid to ask

 The Hyperion Hotel is located at 1481 Hyperion Avenue,
Los Angeles 90036, in the heart of old Hollywood – 68
rooms, 68 vacancies, telephone 213-555-0162. After a
dark and chequered history it will eventually become the
offices for the Angel Investigations team (and the accom-
modation for some).

 Given that dark and chequered past, it's surprising that
Angel doesn't need a full-time exorcist on the staff.
Although, to be fair, Wesley is fairly handy in that department ('I've Got You Under My Skin'). But, if those walls
could talk they would have some truly disturbing tales to
tell.

 Built in 1928, the Hyperion is a rather impressive edifice of
Californian–Spanish architecture with art-deco influences.
It was once a ritzy, glitzy hangout for the movers and shak-
ers of LA. The only problem was that many of the guests
ended up dead and the bills for carpet cleaning had a tendency to lower the management's profit margins.

This was because, unbeknown to the developers, a Thesulac demon had moved in before the builders moved out and, having driven three construction workers to their deaths, it spent the next 72 years whispering in the ears of the unfortunate guests and feeding on their fear and paranoia.

Hotel staff took increasingly desperate measures to conceal the chaos and the high body count within the Hyperion. The bellhop in 1952, Frank Gilnetz, discovered a novel use for the hotel's meat locker and was eventually arrested and executed for numerous murders.

The hotel finally went out of business on 16 December 1979. On that day the concierge, Roland Meeks, made his morning wake-up calls with a 12-gauge shotgun. However, one unfortunate resident stayed on with only the demon for company until 21 years later.

Angel was, briefly, a guest at the hotel in 1952, staying in room 217 and scaring the living bejesus out of the staff. There, he met Judy Kovacs, a woman with many secrets. Not only was Judy a bank robber but she was also of mixed heritage and had been passing as white for many years.

Angel, in a then-rare attempt at connection to humanity, befriended the terrified Judy and attempted to help her. For his pains he was betrayed and handed over to a lynch mob.

Fortunately hanging is one of the ways that you *can't* kill a vampire and Angel escaped. But, disgusted at his treatment, he took the Thesulac demon's advice and left the creature to feast on the insecurities of the remaining guests.

However, nearly 50 years later Angel, in need of a new home and office, becomes interested in the now abandoned and decaying hotel (currently in the hands of Melman Realty & Development group). He finds that the Thesulac demon is still in residence and, indeed, that the unfortunate Judy – now aged but still ridden by guilt at her actions – is also there.

Angel gives Judy the peace and forgiveness she desperately needs and, having summoned and dealt with the demon, he announces to his somewhat startled team that they have found their new home ('Are You Now or Have You Ever Been?').

Despite recovering Judy's ill-gotten gains in the basement, Angel can only afford to lease the hotel for six months with an option to buy. In need of financial advice, he enlists the help of David Nabbit, geek and dotcom billionaire. It seems that if you have no money and want to purchase a 68-room hotel, you need FHA with PMI to cover the down.

When Cordelia is reluctantly pressed into service to clean the hotel she complains bitterly about the dust. However, substances far worse than this will rather frequently need to be removed from the premises in the future.

Presumably the Hyperion's cupboards are well stocked with the appropriate cleaning products to keep the lobby floors sparkling because it'll take more than a mop and bucket to tackle, for instance:

- Ritual pentagrams ('Forgiving').

181

- Desiccated clients ('The Price').

- Dripping ichor ('Fredless').

- Demon guts and entrails ('Quickening').

- Whatever kind of mess that you get left with when you dismember a demon with a chainsaw ('Shiny Happy People').

- Maggoty godlike beings and panicking acolytes ('Peace Out').

 Working for Angel Investigations seems to be a rather dirty job, on both an actual and a metaphorical level. Luckily, there's a washer/dryer in the basement ('The Trial') and, presumably, a plentiful supply of bathrooms, hotel towels and those little bars of soap.

 One hopes that Angel also found enough cash for running repairs or that Wesley and Gunn have hidden talents as builders, handymen and glaziers. Because, frankly, Angel Investigations' clients tend to be a tad hard on the fabric of the building.

 Possible insurance claims include:

- Replacing windows telekinetically shattered by an abuse victim ('Untouched').

- General tidying up after male staff members go on a misogynistic wrecking spree ('Billy').

- Earthquake damage ('Loyalty'). Though it would appear that Angel is lacking in earthquake insurance, so he may have to pay for that one himself ('Sleep Tight').

- Inter-dimensional portals opening in the lobby ('A New World').

Plus, of course, the day-to-day damage caused by battle, torture, murder and mayhem.

One thing is certain: whoever does Angel's maintenance work is highly efficient ... all of the broken windows, for example, seem to be repaired within a week ('Dear Boy'). Perhaps we can add glazier to Wesley's CV of skills.

However, it is noticeable that once Wesley leaves the team his colleagues have great difficulty in coping with a spot of earthquake damage. And, to be frank, the standard of what work they do is pretty amateurish. Mr Wyndam-Pryce is, evidently, a man of many hidden talents and a pretty impressive tool-kit.

But it's not all gloom and doom. The Groosalugg proves to have a surprising grasp of interior décor, firmly advising Angel against decorating in Pomegranate Mist since Sunburst Splendour or purple are hues far more appropriate for the home of a champion ('The Price').

However good the maintenance team may be, the Hyperion is still manifestly in need of some significant structural attention since, according to Wolfram & Hart's Gavin Park, it is in breach of no less than 57 building codes, including asbestos and termites ('That Vision Thing'). Not to mention the rats in the basement ('The Price'). Luckily, Lilah Morgan sorts out the paperwork and Angel Investigations stays in business.

Not even an evil lawyer can fix the perplexing issue of the hotel's location, however. The Hyperion has a 323 area telephone code, which is in Downtown LA despite the fact that Angel claims it to be located in Hollywood in which case it should have a 213 code ('Are You Now or Have You Ever Been?'). Maybe geography isn't his strong point ('Carpe Noctem').

With so many rooms to choose from it's not surprising that Angel sometimes decides on a change of scenery, moving from room 312 ('Dad') to 208 ('Double or Nothing').

He also has a somewhat basic gym – seemingly in the basement – for those times when he needs to get into training for a spot of mayhem ('Redefinition'). Of course, he could use the swimming pool or go for a waltz in the ballroom but maybe that's not quite as butch and manly ('The Price').

It appears that the Hyperion's clientele were sometimes a little careless with the contents of their pockets as Angel finds $1.83 in loose change among the couch cushions ('Provider'). Not quite as impressive as the bagful of stolen cash which, seemingly, was overlooked by generations of builders, maintenance men, hotel staff, estate agents and vandals.

It isn't clear what happened to the Hyperion after the Angel Investigations team moved to the considerably more salubrious environs of Wolfram & Hart but one thing is clear: the two years during which Angel and his team were based there were among the most eventful of the building's long and somewhat disturbing history ('Home').

THROUGH THE LOOKING GLASS

A 'What's On' guide to the fairytale kingdom of Pylea

Looking for an exotic break? Want to astound your family and amaze your friends? Why not choose Pylea as your holiday destination? With its lush green landscapes and dual suns, you're just a short portal-ride away from paradise. Or, whatever afterlife your belief system endorses.

Hunting
Pylea has lots of wildlife. Prove your manhood by joining a Drakken hunt – bring your own thromide-dipped weapon – or, for the truly adventurous, why not take part in an optional excursion to the Scum Pits of Urr where you can engage in unarmed combat with the rare Mogfan beast?

If you prefer a rather less-fatal option, you can hire a Seekul beast and hunt for escaped cow-slaves. Alternatively, if you happen to be human, you can have the thrill of being hunted yourself, at no extra cost.

Nightlife
Although Pyleans have no concept of music *per se*, their nightlife is rich and varied. Watch the legendary Numfar of the Deathwok Clan dance the dance of joy in your honour.

Join in a traditional Backnaal where, as an honoured feast guest, you may be invited to swing the crebbil.

Listen to traditional tales of heroism and adventure or, if you're feeling in the mood for something more lively, why not challenge the reigning champion, the Groosalugg, to a duel? (Funeral arrangements are included in the price of your holiday package.)

Food and drink

Pylean food is simple but plentiful. Cow is a traditional dish, though vegetarians may prefer to sample the local porridge made of crugg-grains, thistles and kalla berries. (Our restaurant critic strongly suggests that you avoid the tree-bark enchiladas.) To round off the evening, why not visit the Hall of Drink and Chance for a refreshing nightcap?

(**Note:** Don't be tempted to drink too much of the local brew and be aware of the possibility of gender confusion and anatomical incompatibilities. And, always be sure to practise safe com-shucking.)

What to wear in Pylea

If you wish to blend in with local customs then please bear in mind that polyester is very definitely frowned upon. Burlap or leather are better choices for the intrepid traveller. (Check out our discount vouchers for Cave Girl's House of Burlap.)

You will need sturdy footwear for the rocky terrain and maybe a fur cloak to keep out the chill of those icy Pylean evenings. Accessorise with the weapons of your choice and complete your look with a fabulous Pylean neck collar, so electrifyingly beautiful it'll blow your mind.

Shopping
The market place in Pylea is great for stocking up on life's little luxuries at bargain prices; take the unique opportunity to fill your basket with delightful local produce such as viper's milk, hefroot, queeks and flib-liquor. With a little haggling you could even bring home a cow as a souvenir of your visit. The more talkative the cow, the lower the price.

(**Note:** Import subject to inter-dimensional customs regulations.)

Culture
Pylea is a non-pluralist, multicultural society with engagingly medieval traditions. The landscape is replete with charming rural villages, impressive palaces and imposing dungeons. No Pylean holiday is complete without a trip to the Mutilation Chambers at the Royal Palace or a visit to a genuine Pylean farm where you will be welcome to try your hand at traditional agriculture and to help out with the care of valuable Flehegna beasts.

(**Note for Vampires:** Since both of Pylea's suns are of the non-fatal variety, vantals can enhance their holiday experience by enjoying the sunshine and noticing how much fire they're *not* on. Pylea also offers vampires a unique opportunity to make vital adjustments to their hairstyle and appearance and to let their inner demon run free.)

Pylea: so good, you'll never want to come home. Visit the foreign languages section of your local library today and ask for *SCRSQWRN*. Then prepare for the adventure of a lifetime.

The management accept no responsibility for guest's inability to create a return portal. Or for death, destruction, civil unrest, slavery, mutilation, head-implosion, banishment to the Scum Pits of Urr, being damned to Tarkna, ritual suicide at the sacrificial canyons of Trelinsk or becoming a bizarre Siamese-twin-type hybrid being. We strongly recommend that all guests take out additional insurance cover available from Wolfram & Hart. By order of the Covenant of Trimboli (all rights reserved).

CITY OF ANGEL
Location spotting, LA-style!

 Some filming for 'City Of' took place in the basement car park of the prestigious Argyle Hotel on possibly the most famous street in the world, Sunset Boulevard. This runs into West Hollywood, where it becomes the even more legendary Sunset Strip, a two-mile conglomeration of chic restaurants, expensive hotels and 'you can't come in here dressed like that'-type nightclubs.

It's home to the Comedy Store, the Whisky-a-Go-Go, the Roxy and the Viper Room and, most notoriously, the Sunset Hyatt, the staging area for the wild and lurid antics of several generations of rock stars from Led Zeppelin, the Rolling Stones, the Who and Hawkwind onwards.

 The exterior location used for the Wolfram & Hart offices was the former MGM-UA building in the Sony Pictures Plaza in Culver City.

 Many of the shots of Oz driving around LA during 'In the Dark' were filmed on the Ventura Freeway near the Warner Brothers studios in Burbank and at the Red Line Subway Terminus on Lankershim Boulevard in North Hollywood.

At one point he passes the Orpheum – a splendid downtown cinema with a mix of French Renaissance and Baroque décor, the interior of which was subsequently used in 'Waiting in the Wings'.

The Griffith Observatory, the central location of 'Are You Now or Have You Ever Been?' is a domed Art Deco monument on the southern slope of Mount Hollywood, it commands a stunning view of the Los Angeles basin below and the Hollywood sign to the right.

A gift to the city by Griffith J Griffith (1850–1919), the Observatory is a perennial favourite of Hollywood filmmakers, best known as the location for the climax of Nicholas Ray's *Rebel Without a Cause* (a bronze bust of James Dean is one of the site's icons). It has also featured in *The Terminator* and *Bowfinger*.

The premises used for Denver's shop in 'Are You Now or Have You Ever Been?' and 'Reprise' was the legendary Hollywood Book City store on Hollywood Boulevard.

The location used for exterior shots of the Hyperion was the Los Altos Hotel and Apartments, built in 1925 and situated on Wilshire Boulevard.

Many of the Hyperion's interiors in both 'Billy' and 'The Price' were filmed in the abandoned Ambassador Hotel in downtown LA.

The sequence in which Cordelia and Gunn bitch at each other while driving in 'First Impressions' was filmed in Burbank and Magnolia Boulevard in North Hollywood

191

(best known as the setting for Paul Thomas Anderson's 1999 travelogue in human misery *Magnolia*). Some of the shots of Wesley and Angel riding on the motorbike were filmed on Ventura Boulevard in Sherman Oaks.

The Promenade used in 'Dear Boy' is in Santa Monica on Third Street, an open-air pedestrian boardwalk with restaurants, shops, movie theatres and nightclubs.

One of the most desirable places to live in LA, Santa Monica is most famous for its pier, the luxurious state beach and Third Street Promenade. Not forgetting the numerous bars on Santa Monica Boulevard itself, immortalised in Sheryl Crow's 'All I Wanna Do'. It's also home to the Mutant Enemy production lot where most of *Buffy* and some of *Angel* were filmed. Santa Monica has certainly changed since Raymond Chandler used it as the setting for *Farewell My Lovely* and described it as resembling a giant funfair.

The shooting location for Jenoff's establishment in 'Double or Nothing' was Larry Flynt's Hustler Casino outside Los Angeles.

In 'I Will Remember You', when Buffy meets Angel, the scene was filmed against the backdrop of the Santa Monica Pier and Pacific Park. The latter itself was used as a location in 'Loyalty'.

The magnificent view of downtown LA from the rooftop nursery in 'Reunion' includes shots of the One Wilshire Boulevard building, the City National Bank on West 5th Street and a sign for the Hotel Haywood Café on West 6th

Street. Angel and friends are also seen driving along Hollywood Boulevard past the Fox Theater.

 The Romanian street scenes in 'Five by Five' were shot at Universal Studios' Little Europe, as were the Italian exteriors in 'The Girl in Question'.

 One of the locations used for 'Long Day's Journey' was an oil refinery situated close to Jefferson Boulevard, south of Downtown LA. The same site was also used for a memorable sequence in the first season of *24*.

 The building used for Billy Blim's home in 'Billy' was one owned by former Los Angeles Mayor Richard Riordon.

 Several publications have stated that in 'Lullaby' Angel finds Darla on the roof of the Hollywood Roosevelt Hotel. In actual fact, the hotel used was the Rosslyn on Main Street in the Skid Row area.

 Some of the filming for 'Shiny Happy People' took place on Mulholland Drive, bordering Griffith Park. From its starting point near the 101 Freeway to its terminus at LA County's Pacific boundary, Mulholland twists for 21 miles through mountain passes and canyons, offering extraordinary views of LA to the south and the Valley to the north.

The road passes through the Hollywood Hills and is famous for the numerous celebrities who've had homes on or near it. (These include Elvis Presley who, in August 1965, had his only meeting with the Beatles there.) Mulholland has also been immortalised in songs (REM's 'Electrolyte') and movies (David Lynch's *Mulholland Drive*).

TEENAGE KICKS

The moody and somewhat sullen story of a boy called
Connor

Kids, eh? They grow up so fast these days; it seems like only yesterday that snarling feral teenage berserker was a bouncing baby boy having his nappy changed.

Of course, in the case of Connor, it *was* only yesterday.

 Connor's conception and birth were, seemingly, miraculous. The child of two vampires born amid violence, death and mayhem in a rain-swept alley, Connor certainly had an unusual start to his life ('Lullaby'). For one thing, at less than one day old he already had an enemies list: a vampire sect wished to worship him; Wolfram & Hart wanted to dissect him and a transdimensional demon wanted him dead ('Dad').

 Then there was the small matter of a resurrected vampire hunter out for revenge on Connor's parents ('Provider') and a tricky little prophecy that seemed to suggest Angel would kill his own son ('Loyalty'). However, Connor was a much loved and much wanted child and the Angel Investigations team doted on him. To such an extent that when Wesley discovered the fake prophecy he was prepared to risk everything he had to keep the child safe.

Angel and his friends were therefore devastated when Holtz gained his revenge by transporting the infant Connor to Quor-Toth, darkest of the demon dimensions, where Connor would be raised to hate Angel and all that he stood for ('Sleep Tight').

Unsurprisingly, it was a somewhat mixed blessing when Connor returned from Quor-Toth. For one thing, he was no longer a baby but a feral teenage warrior. Also, Holtz's plan had been devastatingly successful and Connor was bent on revenge against his blood father. When his first attempt at patricide failed, Connor found himself alone in a bewildering new world. It certainly wasn't the ideal introduction to modern life and, for all his attitude, Connor found it a highly traumatic experience ('A New World').

Despite his many problems, Connor soon seemed to adapt to Los Angeles, fighting alongside his father and getting to know the Angel Investigations team. Left to himself, it was perfectly possible that Connor would have eventually adapted to his new surroundings. However, Holtz had not yet finished with his vengeance and managed to stage his own death in such a way that Connor believed Angel to be responsible ('Benediction').

A grief-stricken Connor vowed revenge and plotted to destroy Angel, sealing him in a coffin and sinking him to the bottom of the ocean ('Tomorrow'). Connor then returned to the Hyperion and to the care of the unsuspecting Gunn and Fred.

When his perfidy is eventually exposed, a furious Fred administers some much needed discipline in the form of a taser blast before a rescued Angel tells his son that he loves him and then throws him out of the hotel ('Deep Down'). However, Angel continues to keep a watchful eye on his errant offspring ('Ground State').

Connor soon finds a friend in the form of an amnesic Cordelia, returned from a higher plane without her memory. Cordy feels comfortable with Connor and moves in with him to his somewhat dingy squat above a warehouse ('Slouching Towards Bethlehem'). Their relationship quickly takes on a rather disturbing element as the pair kiss ('Supersymmetry'). Then, after The Beast rises from the exact spot where Connor was born and as fire rains down on Los Angeles, Cordy takes Connor to her bed, unaware that Angel is watching ('Apocalypse Nowish'). However, Angel manages to keep his anger and disgust under control and even rescues Connor from the newly devastated offices of Wolfram & Hart before telling Cordelia to take her new boyfriend and get the hell out of his sight ('Habeas Corpses').

Worse is to follow as a bemused Connor discovers that he is to become a father. And with rather less than the usual nine months waiting time to adjust to the idea. He also has to deal with the ramifications of Cordelia's new status as an agent of evil. Such is his love of, and loyalty towards, Cordy that he stands by her and rescues her from the right-eous anger of the Angel Investigations team ('Players').

He then allows a possessed and clearly insane Cordelia to convince him that they don't have to live by society's rules and that, as their child's life is in danger, they must procure a virgin sacrifice to complete a ritual that will induce the birth. Connor obliges and, despite the attempted intervention of his dead mother, he slits the terrified girl's throat and uses her blood to induce a mystical labour. Angel arrives to kill the woman he loves and thus save the world but he finds himself unable to do so and, as Jasmine is born, Connor and Angel fall to their knees and worship her ('Inside Out').

The messianic Jasmine has come to save the world from itself and Connor is a more than willing disciple. Jasmine tells the bedazzled boy that Angel and Darla were specifically chosen to be his parents and that he, himself, was created to father her and thus help to rid the world of evil ('Shiny Happy People').

As Connor bonds with his father and the pair sing duets to Jasmine's praise, he reveals that Holtz taught him how to track people in Quor-Toth at around five years of age. Holtz would tie him to a tree and Connor would have to free himself and track Holtz down. His personal best was five days. It's therefore no wonder that the lad has some issues. Meanwhile, Fred – who can see Jasmine's true face and has thus become a hunted outcast – is working on a plan to mix Jasmine's blood with that of the team members. Her ploy works on everyone except, seemingly, Connor ('The Magic Bullet').

The team are forced to flee from the wrath of Jasmine's followers while Connor, still utterly faithful to Jasmine, joins in the pursuit until his father punches him unconscious and throws him from a building. Jasmine pauses in her people-eating to heal a bruised and battered Connor and to reassure him that all will be well if he only surrenders to her completely and lets go of the pain that has been the only constant in his life. Then, channelling Jasmine, Connor leads an army against his former friends ('Sacrifice').

It seems that Connor has been able to see Jasmine's true face all along, but he finds it beautiful. Strange child, but then he *did* grow up in a Hell dimension. However, the captured Wesley, Gunn, Fred and Lorne have put some doubts in Connor's mind. He goes in search of Cordelia and pours out his confused heart to her comatose form. Connor explains that he has tried to believe and he wants to feel the peace and love of Jasmine but he can't stop fighting or let go of his hate and anger. His entire life has been built on lies but he thought that this lie was, frankly, better than most of the others.

It is Connor who, ultimately, kills Jasmine as her empire of peace and love crashes into chaos. Then he flees into the night, leaving Angel to worry about his son's state of mind ('Peace Out'). A conflicted Connor wanders the city, becoming increasingly disturbed until finally he snaps, first beating up a suicidal policeman because he was going to desert his family and then wiring himself up as a human bomb and holding innocent shoppers hostage. His problem, it seems, is not that he has lost the perfect peace and love of Jasmine but that he never felt it in the first place. He is cold, incapable of emotion and his life has no meaning. Worst of all, he blames Angel for letting Holtz take him to Hell and make him what he has become. The only true thing, Connor believes, is death – everything else is just a lie, and you can't be saved by a lie.

Angel is forced to – apparently – kill his son to save him from himself. But, secretly, he has made a deal with Wolfram & Hart to give Connor a new life and to erase all the unhappy memories of his time as Angel's son. In return, Angel is given a brief glimpse of a happy Connor safe with his new family and about to go to college ('Home').

However, all does not go quite as planned and Angel is disturbed when Connor's adoptive parents turn up in the offices of Wolfram & Hart. It seems that Connor's new life is not quite as normal as it's supposed to be. Connor has retained his superstrength and was able to survive a hit-and-run attack unscathed. He also, apparently, has enemies who want him dead.

At first Angel refuses to have anything to do with the case but, having saved Connor's parents from a demon attack – and earned Connor's respect and admiration in the process – he changes his mind. Connor, now a Stanford college student, is fascinated by the offices of Wolfram & Hart and especially enthralled by the charms of Illyria; it seems that the mind-wipe spell didn't cure him of his somewhat unhealthy penchant for older women.

Angel learns that the demons who attacked Connor's parents were minions of the warlock Cyvus Vail. Cyvus 'created' Connor's new life and memories and now he wants Connor to fulfil an ancient prophecy and kill his old enemy Sahjhan. In return Vail will keep the mind-wipe spell intact and leave Connor and his family alone and blissfully ignorant of the truth. Angel trains Connor to defeat Sahjhan but Wesley, alerted by Illyria to the fact that the team's memories have been altered, breaks the Orlon window that contains the original past. As the spell is broken Connor regains memories of his past life and it is the angry, vicious destroyer buried deep within him who kills Sahjhan, rather than the bright and pacifist young man whom Connor has become in his new life ('Origin').

Although Connor remains with his adoptive parents, he acknowledges Angel as his real father and the pair begin to build a new relationship. It is with Connor that Angel chooses to spend what will probably be his last day on Earth and Connor helps Angel in his fight against Marcus Hamilton.

Connor's old life and new memories have blended and he seems to be a remarkably well-adjusted young man. He is concerned about his father's fight against Wolfram & Hart but Angel sends him home, assuring him that as long as he knows that Connor is safe nothing can destroy him.

The wild, conflicted young man has become a son that any father would be proud of ('Not Fade Away').

LOGIC, LET ME INTRODUCE YOU TO THIS WINDOW (PART 2)

More things in *Angel* that make absolutely no logical sense whatsoever

 There are two different models of Philco refrigerators used in Angel's apartment during Season 1. One – seen in 'Rm W/a Vu' – is squarish, with the makers name across the door. The other model (seen in other first-season episodes) is rounded, with the name near the handle.

 If Doyle and Harry married before they were 20 – 'The Bachelor Party' – then how could Doyle have been teaching third grade when they met at such a young age?

 In 'Somnambulist', when Penn refers to Angel not meeting him in Italy he says he waited 'until the nineteenth century'. Angel gives his reason as getting held up in Romania, which took place in 1898, so surely Penn must mean the *twentieth* century?

 Everyone's bruises go through startling changes throughout 'Sanctuary'. Faith's, for instance, vacillate between raw and nearly invisible then back again. Also, the cut on

Buffy's lip from Angel's punch disappears entirely in one scene, only to reappear later.

A medieval-style joust happens in the middle of downtown LA with a tribunal of black-clad judges and two guys on horseback in 'Judgment', and no one seems to notice. Some fans have suggested the whole thing is mystical and therefore not noticeable to anyone not involved (obscured behind a Joyce Summers-style denial shield no doubt). It's still a hell of a contrivance. Maybe everyone thought it was a movie shoot?

Lindsey drives over Angel in a truck three times and then smashes him repeatedly in the face with a sledgehammer in 'Epiphany'. This causes *a bit of minor bruising* and nothing else.

In 'There's No Place Like Plrtz Glrb', Sasha appears to be watching the fight between Angel and the Groosalugg (he's standing directly behind Fred). Then, several seconds later, he *arrives* with the group that includes Wesley, Gunn and Cordelia to stop the battle.

The Furies appear to *know* Angel in the biblical sense ('That Old Gang of Mine'). We must therefore assume that it takes more than fantastic sex with three celestial beings to make him *truly* happy.

Could Justine and Connor get all the materials that they needed to send Angel to his watery grave (a boat, a metal coffin, welding equipment) in such a short space of time? It takes some believing that they arranged everything in the hour or so after Connor learned that Angel would be meeting Cordy near the ocean. Additionally, where did Connor learn how to use a power tool so effectively? Come to that, Justine's sudden acquisition of welding skills is also a bit suspicious ('Tomorrow').

 General fifth season query: if everybody has forgotten about Connor and everything related to him (see 'Home') then how does Wesley believe Cordelia got into her coma? For that matter, does Lorne remember why Caritas was destroyed for a second time (see 'Quickening')? Do all the gang remember Darla, or Jasmine, or any of the other events that directly included Connor during the last two years of their lives?

There is an attempt to answer this in 'Origin', but it's only partly successful. Wesley can clearly remember Angel's previous battles with Sahjhan, noting that Angel nearly died during the last one ('Forgiving'). Despite this, until the Orlon Window is smashed, he's unable to remember Connor's significant role in those events.

The implication seems to be that, in the revised timeline, events still happened more or less as they did before, just without Connor being a part of them. Therefore, Darla still came back and still killed herself, only for a different reason than saving her unborn son. Holtz still jumped through the dimensional portal to Quor-Toth. Wesley still turned to the dark side, but for a different reason than his guilt over betraying Angel by kidnapping his son.

And, presumably, it was someone else who copulated with Cordelia to produce Jasmine. It would be a brave production, however, that would have attempted to address some of these anomalies because the entire concept is the kind of thing that looks good on paper but, when you start to pick at it, the whole thing can come to pieces in your hands like wet cardboard.

For instance, what other issue would temporarily ensoul Darla to the extent that she achieves a motherly redemption through self-sacrifice?

That's a remarkably spacious U-boat in 'Why We Fight'. Anyone who has visited the surviving U-boat (U-995) at the German naval military museum in Laboe can testify as to just how narrow and cramped conditions are on board.

Additionally, no one can get from the forward end of a submarine to the aft without going through the control room – there just isn't an alternative route. Electric power availability for the lights has nothing to do with whether the motors are working.

During the 1943 flashback Spike uses the word 'groovy' a good decade and a half before it properly entered the vocabulary. The first recorded use of the word, surprisingly, occurred as early as 1941. However, in those days it was very much a New Orleans jazz term – meaning 'playing, with inspiration' (from the grooves on a record). During the late 1950s, the US beatnik movement adopted it as a descriptive term for something or someone being attractive, fashionable or exciting and that is the context in which Spike uses it.

Illyria asks Knox in 'Shells' if he is her Qua'ha'xahn. Knox notes that he is her priest, servant and guide to the world. He has taken her sacraments and placed them close to his heart according to the ancient ways. Illyria is dismissive, noting that her last Qua'ha'xahn was taller. But Illyria is from a time before humans even existed ('A Hole in the World', 'Time Bomb'). She then says that she believed humans would have long died out by now. Even the most liberal estimates concerning evolution place the dawn of mankind as considerably more recent than a million years ago.

'MAGIC. YOU PEOPLE RELY TOO MUCH ON THAT JUNK'

12 classic lines of dialogue from *Angel*'s Season 4

- Fred: 'I'm working on a plan. So far, it involves being sent to prison and becoming somebody's bitch.' ('Ground State')

- Gunn: 'Something's starting to feel a lot not-right about this.' Fred: 'That's what I've been saying. Only with better grammar.' ('The House Always Wins')

- Gunn: 'How horrible is this thing?' Lorne: 'I haven't read the Book of Revelations [sic] lately, but if I was searching for adjectives, I'd probably start there.' ('Slouching Towards Bethlehem')

- Lorne: 'No pain, no side effects. I'm telling you, swingers, there is *no way* this can fail. So, I'm an idiot. What are you? Perfect?' ('Spin the Bottle')

- Connor: 'What's a zombie?' Angel: 'An undead thing.' Connor: 'Like you?' Angel: 'No. Zombies are slow, dim-witted things that crave human flesh.' Connor: 'Like you?' ('Habeas Corpses')

- Angel: 'We've done things we're sure can never be forgiven, but we're always there for each other when it counts. We've never let the darkness win … It's because we believe in each other, not just as friends or lovers, but as *Champions*.' ('Awakening')

- Angelus, to Connor: 'Doesn't it freak you out that she used to change your diapers? The first woman you boned is the closest thing you've ever had to a mother. Doin' your mom and trying to kill your dad? There should be a play!' ('Soulless')

- Angelus: 'Aw, *crap*! You mean killing The Beast really *does* bring back the sun? I thought that was Angel's retarded fantasy.' ('Salvage')

- Willow: 'How've you been?' Cordelia: 'Higher Being. You?' Willow: 'Ultimate Evil. I got *better*!' ('Orpheus')

- Wesley, to Angel: 'What do you want to do?' Skip: 'The only thing he can do. Kill the woman he loves and save the world. Times like this, it's really gotta suck being you.' ('Inside Out')

- Angel: 'I didn't say we were smart, I said it's our right. It's what makes us human.' Jasmine: 'You're *not* human.' Angel: 'Workin' on it.' ('Peace Out')

- Gunn: 'You want to give us your evil law firm. We ain't lawyers.' Fred: 'Or *evil*. Currently.' ('Home')

'YOU MAY REMEMBER ME FROM SUCH FILMS AND TV SHOWS AS ...' (PART 2)

15 more familiar guest stars on *Angel*

 Eliza Dushku (Faith) made her film debut aged 11 in *That Night*. She played Emma in *Bye Bye Love*, Missy in *Bring It On*, Dana Tasker in *True Lies* and appeared in *Jay and Silent Bob Strike Back* and *Soul Survivor*.

 Sam Anderson (Holland Manners) was Kevin Davis in *The Cape*, Doctor Keyson in *ER* and the Fonzie-loving doctor who delivered Phoebe's triplets in *Friends*. He also appeared in *Forrest Gump*, *La Bamba*, *The West Wing* and *The X-Files*.

 Juliet Landau (Drusilla), despite appearances in movies such as *The Grifters*, *Pump Up the Volume*, *Theodore Rex* and *Citizens of Perpetual Indulgence* and TV series such as *Parker Lewis Can't Lose* and *La Femme Nikita* is best known for her performance as Loretta King opposite her father in Tim Burton's *Ed Wood*.

 Brigid Brannagh (Virginia Bryce) played Claire in *Hyperion Bay*, Sasha in *Kindred: The Embraced* and Donna in *Dharma & Greg* and has appeared in *The Man in the Iron Mask*, *Sliders*, *Charmed* and *CSI*.

Tony Todd (Vyasa in 'The Shroud of Rahmon') played both Kurn, Worf's brother, and the older Jake Sisko in *Star Trek: Deep Space 9*, Captain Darrow in *The Rock*, Ben in *Night of the Living Dead*, Cecrops in *Xena: Warrior Princess* and the title character in *Candyman* and its sequels.

 Tom McCleister (Lorne's Mother) played Red Wood in *Midnight Run*, Ike on *Married ... with Children*, and was also in *Fletch Lives*, *Twins*, *Cheers*, *Roswell* and *Grosse Pointe*.

 The father of Ron and Clint Howard, Rance Howard (Marcus Roscoe in 'Carpe Noctem') has a CV covering almost 50 years with appearances in *Married ... with Children*, *Seinfeld*, *Dynasty*, *Happy Days*, *Battlestar Galactica*, *The Waltons*, *Kung Fu*, *The Virginian*, *The Andy Griffith Show* and *Perry Mason*. His movies include *Spider-Man*, *Where Truth Lies*, *Apollo 13*, *Ed Wood*, *Parenthood*, *The Executioner's Song*, *Grand Theft Auto* (which he also wrote and produced), *Chinatown*, *Cool Hand Luke* and *The Music Man*.

 John Rubinstein (Linwood Murrow) played Harrison Fox Jr in *Crazy Like a Fox* and appeared in *The Boys from Brazil*, *Cannon*, *Red Dragon*, *Roots: The Next Generation* and *The Car*. The son of piano virtuoso Arthur Rubinstein, John was a composer on series such as *China Beach* and *Harry O*. He also won a Tony in 1980 for his performance in *Children of a Lesser God* and was the original lead in the Broadway production of Bob Fosse's *Pippin*.

 Jim Ortlieb (Vampire Hunter in 'Lullaby') played Nasedo in *Roswell*. His CV also includes a memorable role in *Magnolia* and appearances in *Chain Reaction*, *Home Alone*, *Flatliners*, *Spin City*, *The Shield*, *Felicity* and *Early Edition*.

Simon Templeman is best known as the voice of Kain on the video game series *The Legacy of Kain*. He played the Angel of Death on *Charmed* and appeared in *Live Nude Girls*, *24* and *Star Trek: The Next Generation*.

Born in London in 1923, Roy Dotrice (Roger Wyndam-Pryce in 'Lineage') played Zeus in *Hercules: The Legendary Journeys*, Father in *Beauty and the Beast* and the title role in *Dickens of London*. He provided voice-work on the BBC documentary series *The Ascent of Man* and his CV also includes appearances in *LA Law*, *Space: 1999*, *Babylon 5*, *Hart to Hart*, *Picket Fences*, *Amadeus* and *The Equalizer* opposite his son-in-law Edward Woodward. Roy is the father of actress Michele Dotrice.

Tom Lenk (Andrew Wells) also appeared in *Six Feet Under*, *Boogie Nights* and *Popular*.

Born in Salt Lake City in 1975, Jaime Bergman (Amanda in 'Time Bomb') was the January 1999 *Playboy* Playmate of the Month. She married David Boreanaz in 2000 and the couple have a son, Jaden Rayne. Jaime's acting credits include *Any Given Sunday*, *Dark Wolf*, *Virgins*, *Gone in Sixty Seconds*, *Shasta McNasty* and – her most famous role – BJ Cummings in *Son of the Beach*.

Jack Conley (Sahjhan) often gets meaty detective-type roles in movies such as *Payback*, *Mercury Rising*, *LA Confidential* and *Get Shorty*. He played Cain in *Buffy* and also appeared in *Collateral Damage*, *Traffic* and *Apollo 13*, *NYPD Blue*, *Dark Skies*, *Without a Trace* and *Kindred: The Embraced*.

Dennis Christopher (Cyvus Vail) has been in numerous movies including *Mind Rage*, *Skeletons*, *Doppelgänger*, *The Disco Years*, *Jake Speed*, *Chariots of Fire* (as Charles Paddock), Fellini's *Roma*, *Breaking Away* and *Alien Predator*. On TV he guest-starred in *Moonlighting*, *Freakylinks* and *Star Trek: Deep Space Nine*.

'BIKES, HELICOPTERS AND AUTOMOBILES'

10 Methods of transportation used by characters in *Angel*

 Angel initially drives a black 1968 Plymouth Belvedere GTX convertible – NKD 714 ('City of'). It is, as the T'ish Magev notes, a complete gas hog but, probably, a chick magnet ('Guise Will Be Guise'). Angel can also drive a motorcycle ('Hero').

 Wesley drives a rather impressive Big Dog motorcycle ('Parting Gifts', 'First Impressions', 'Unleashed'). At some point, however, he acquired a Cherokee Jeep (licence 3QTI895), which Justine steals after slitting Wes's throat ('Sleep Tight').

 Unsurprisingly, Wolfram & Hart own the biggest black limo you have probably ever seen, along with a green Isuzu truck used to transport crates containing the recently Hell-raised ('To Shanshu in LA').

 Lindsey drives a silver Mercedes C55-class with licence plate 3210879 ('Darla'). However, when he leaves LA, he's driving a Real Man's 1956 Ford F-100 pickup with Oklahoma licence plate T-42633 ('Dead End'), which goes magnificently with his whup-ass boots.

When Gunn was 17, he offered to trade his soul to the demon casino-owner Jenoff in exchange for the truck that he still drives. Fred is astonished that his soul, seemingly, wasn't worth air-conditioning as an optional extra ('War Zone', 'Double or Nothing').

 On taking over Wolfram & Hart, not only does Angel discover that he owns numerous classic cars – much to his obvious delight – but he also has access to a private helicopter ('Conviction'). One of Angel's new cars is a stunning 1991 Dodge Viper ('Just Rewards'). It's the very same car that Spike steals to drive off in search of the Cup of Perpetual Torment ('Destiny') and it's also, quite possibly, the car that Spike has just crashed when he turns up demanding another one ('Smile Time').

 Nina drives a 1992 Honda Civic – 2ABM-543 ('Unleashed').

 Angel, Spike and Gunn take the company's Chevrolet Camaro SS on their rescue mission to find Lindsey in the Wolfram & Hart holding dimension. The car, it appears, can navigate itself towards (and through) dimensional portals ('Underneath').

 Escaping from the Rome club, having stolen the Capo di Famiglia's head, Alfonso also appropriates Angel and Spike's – presumably hired – Ferrari. The vampires duly follow him on a Vespa scooter ('The Girl in Question').

 According to Knox, Wolfram & Hart's *really* good' aeroplanes can get from Los Angeles to England in just four hours ('A Hole in the World', 'Shells').

ANGEL AND SPIKE (DECEASED)

The singular story of the (allegedly) ambiguously gay duo

Having been cursed with a soul, Angel brooded for a century, repenting his dreadful crimes until, eventually, he was persuaded to go to Sunnydale to help the Slayer Buffy Summers and her friends in the war on terror. The pair fell in love but Angel's gypsy curse had a nasty hidden clause: a single moment of perfect happiness and he would lose his soul again. Angel, realising that he could not provide Buffy with the life that she deserved, moved to Los Angeles to continue the fight against evil ('City Of').

As a human in 1880, William was a sensitive (if somewhat bloody awful) poet who was belittled and ridiculed by his peers and by Cecily Underwood, the woman whom he unrequitedly cherished. However, a chance meeting with Drusilla up a dark alleyway changed all that and William began his metamorphosis into Spike, one of the most fearsome vampires on record ('Fool for Love'). Having killed two Slayers in the following century, Spike would ultimately (and unexpectedly) fall madly in love with a third and, thus, embark on a path that would lead to him regaining his soul and sacrificing himself to save the world.

Spike and his grandsire Angel have shared much over the years. It was Angel who taught the young William about life as a vampire. Spike's very existence is a constant reminder to Angel of his own evil past. As Spike perceptively notes, Drusilla may have made him a vampire but it was Angel who made him a monster and every time Angel looks at Spike he sees all the nasty things he, himself, has done ('Destiny').

 Spike, meanwhile, has seemingly never missed an opportunity to rub Angel's rhubarb, constantly taunting him about his sexuality, his broodiness and, regularly, his haircut, having him tortured ('In the Dark') and inadvertently ruining an opportunity to get his curse reversed by eating the gypsies Darla was trying to use as a bargaining tool ('Darla'). It was also Spike's conspiracy with Buffy that led directly to Angel being sent to Hell for a few hundred years and whose subsequent relationship with the Slayer really pissed Angel off. In short, this pair have history.

 The duo seem, at first glance, to cordially detest each other with a vengeance. But there is acceptance, comradeship, even a kind of love beneath the sarcastic, bitter surface. In many ways the relationship is brotherly, Spike having modelled himself on Angelus. Spike, it's fair to speculate, looked up to him, once hailing Angel as 'my Yoda'. Spike continually seems to wish to emulate Angel, coveting – and getting – his cars, his lifestyle, and even his women.

 On a more pragmatic note, almost everything about Spike irritates Angel. The pair, quite simply, get on each other's nerves and indulge in a constant exchange of bitching and bickering. However, when the chips are down they fight

215

together for a common cause and it is Spike who is first to raise his hand and volunteer for almost certain death at the hands of The Circle Of The Black Thorn ('Not Fade Away').

Perhaps the biggest difference between the souled Spike and Angel is that while Angel, seemingly, has two entirely different personas – Angelus being his evil side and Angel the part of him who is seeking redemption – Spike sees no distinction between his past crimes and his present redemption. Instead, he takes responsibility for his years of mayhem, refusing to accept that he is a different person now.

When the insane Slayer Dana takes a terrible revenge on him for killing her family – an act of which he was innocent – Spike remarks that he has killed a lot of people's families and thus the punishment is deserved ('Damage'). In fact, both vampires killed their own parents – Angel as an act of revenge, Spike when an attempt to give his mother eternal life went terribly wrong.

Angel lives a guilt-stricken existence, obsessed by his past sins, whereas Spike would rather rescue the girl (particularly if there was some emerald stealing involved in the scenario) and then go and share a bottle of hooch and listen to the Sex Pistols.

Spike envies Angel's circle of friends and somewhat luxurious lifestyle. Angel, meanwhile, is thoroughly irritated that while he was cursed with a soul and spent a century brooding and eating rats, Spike seems to have adjusted after only a few weeks of mild insanity in a Sunnydale basement. Sometimes life just isn't fair.

Both men seek redemption but, in their heart of hearts, both believe that atonement is ultimately impossible and that their eventual destination is to be Hell and damnation. When Angel tells Fred that some people simply can't be saved, he is referring as much to himself as to his wayward grandson. Still, Spike takes comfort from the fact that at least he'll have Angel for company in the afterlife ('Hellbound').

 The biggest bone of contention between the pair is, of course, Buffy – the Slayer whom both men loved and lost. Lorne sees the potential of this as an epic screenplay starring Johnny Depp and Orlando Bloom. But then, Lorne spends *a lot* of time thinking about those two anyway. Angel says, angrily, that his and Buffy's love is forever. Spike reminds Angel that *he* had a relationship with Buffy too. Sleeping together is not a relationship, replies Angel. It is if you do it enough times, argues Spike ('The Girl in Question').

 Angel's love for Buffy ultimately cost him his soul and led to an extended period in a hell dimension. Spike, meanwhile, fought to become a better man and when he realised that he needed a soul to be worthy of Buffy, he went to Africa and got one.

 Crucially, Spike's soul comes without the pesky happiness curse that Angel's is attached to. It's no wonder Angel is peeved to the point of petulance about Spike's relationship with Buffy or that he, conveniently, forgets to tell his team that he is no longer the only souled vampire in existence.

He is also less than pleased when Buffy sends him back to LA and chooses Spike as her champion in her final battle with The First Evil. And, thus, Angel plays down Spike's subsequent role in averting the apocalypse. In the final analysis, Angel's love for Buffy nearly caused the end of the world, while Spike's love and sacrifice *saved* the world. The child has finally become the father of the man and that's got to sting.

Angel's fury when a resurrected Spike appears in his office is, therefore, entirely understandable. Spike is also less than thrilled at the situation, believing himself to have landed in Hell even before he realises that he's become, effectively, a ghost. As he aptly remarks, 'Bugger!' ('Just Rewards').

From Spike's first appearance in LA, he makes Angel's life an utter misery. In his ghostly form he's forever popping up at inconvenient moments. Plus, his very presence distracts the Angel Investigations team from their work as Fred focuses much of her energies on recorporealising Spike at vast cost to the organisation (' Hellbound').

However, despite the constant bickering and Spike's status as a reluctant wisecracking ghostly sidekick, the pair do work together and even spend some quality time talking of a past where Angel secretly enjoyed William's poetry. But then, as Spike points out, Angel also liked Barry Manilow, so that's really no recommendation.

Once Spike has his body back, he decides to leave LA. However, Angel doesn't seem too keen to help in this endeavour and Spike soon has second thoughts, fearing that his resurrection will somehow diminish his noble sacrifice in Buffy's eyes. And, when it becomes clear that Spike's presence as a second souled champion is causing major disruption to the universe, Angel asks him to stay.

The subsequent battle to establish once and for all which of them is the true champion brings many simmering issues to the fore as the pair recall past triumphs and betrayals. Tellingly, when Spike has the opportunity to stake Angel he chooses to spare him, ostensibly because he doesn't want Buffy moaning about it ('Destiny').

The pair return to Wolfram & Hart with a new respect for each other and, in Angel's case, a dawning fear that, maybe, Spike *is* the true champion after all and it will be Spike and not he who receives the reward of the Shanshu prophecy. This fear is heightened as Spike seemingly takes on Angel's role as helper of the helpless. A series of parasite-induced hallucinations reveals just how deep-seated Angel's insecurities are as he sees Spike saving the world, receiving the respect and adoration of the team and, ultimately, being given the gift of humanity ('Soul Purpose').

Spike's arrival causes Angel to question everything that he believed in and worked towards with regard to his own destiny. It takes a seemingly supernatural visit from his old friend Cordelia to put him back on the right path ('You're Welcome').

The adversaries do manage to put aside their differences when the mission demands, jetting to England to visit the Deeper Well in a desperate effort to save Fred, and comforting each other when the mission, ultimately, fails. Crucially, in this situation it is Spike who has the cooler

219

head, pausing on the bridge to poetically allow Angel to understand that the price demanded for Fred's life is one that they cannot pay ('A Hole in the World').

From a thorn in Angel's side, Spike has become a valued member of the team (which is not to say that his advice is always welcomed or appreciated). And tellingly, when a timeslip lets him alter history, Angel unhesitatingly allows himself to be painfully, if non-fatally, staked to save Spike from certain death at the hands of Illyria ('Time Bomb').

Angel would far rather Spike not get involved in a mission to reclaim the head of the Capo di Famiglia in Rome. But, once Spike learns that Buffy is in the clutches of The Immortal, the vilest evil that Hell ever spewed forth, there is no stopping him. The duo's inept attempts to complete the mission *and* to save their girl – who, seemingly, has no wish to be saved – convinces them both, in theory at least, that they need to move on and to consign their relationships with Buffy to the past.

Andrew tries to explain that Buffy loves them both and may at some point choose one of them to spend the rest of her life with but, in the meantime, they have no option but to return to LA and get on with their own lives. Angel moves on, finding affection in the arms of the werewolf girl Nina, while Spike seems to make a real effort to become a part of the team ('Power Play').

The final battle sees Spike and Angel living out one last day. Angel chooses to send Nina away from the conflict and to spend some time with his son, Connor. Spike, meanwhile, dusts off some old ambitions and attends a poetry slam where, finally, his *Ode to Cecily* is greeted with respect (and, indeed, adulation). As he acknowledges the applause of the crowd it seems that William the Poet has finally found the acceptance he has been seeking for so long.

So they stand together – with their friends – in yet another wet alley facing insurmountable odds and fighting on the side of good. Two champions. Two legends ('Not Fade Away').

221

WHO'S THE HARDEST?

If all the main villains from *Angel* had a massive fight, which
of them would win?

Lindsey McDonald
Introduced as a generic hate-figure in the opening episode.
Thereafter, far too often, Lindsey is compromised either by
some pesky residual spark of humanity within him ('Blind
Date') or by his doomed love for a bad vampire ('Darla').
Something that even the unlikely acquisition of an evil
hand couldn't put right ('Dead End').

He survived the *Groundhog Day*-style horrors of a
Wolfram & Hart holding dimension, however
('Undefeated'), so he's clearly got some spunk about him.
But, ultimately, it's his dying words to Lorne ('Not Fade
Away') that define Lindsey's weakness: it was always sup-
posed to be his nemesis, Angel, that killed him, not some
mere flunky.

Lilah Morgan
Like Lindsey, Lilah's survival within Wolfram & Hart
depended on developing a thick skin, a manipulative way
with others, an ability to lie one's way out of virtually any
situation and a fondness for dropping one's knickers to

gain both information and pleasure. All things that Lilah does *magnificently*. Particularly the latter.

Sadly, the girl's a waste of space when it comes to actually killing people herself rather than getting someone else to do it (see, for example, 'Calvary'). Although 'Billy' does, at least, prove she has *some* backbone for dirty jobs.

Darla and Drusilla

The ladies who, let's remember, *ate* most of the Contracts Department at Wolfram & Hart. They've got the looks, the attitude, the experience and the really satisfying ability to exterminate homophobic scumbags ('Reunion').

Add in a load of unresolved, and really complicated, parental issues ('Redefinition'), their only – possibly fatal – compromise is their close and personal relationship to Angel. But if vampires with souls aren't involved in any face-off then these, frankly, are your girls.

The Covenant of Trimboli

Pfft. Lightweight Spanish Inquisition clones whose total power and domination over Pylean society comes, largely, from the ignorance of the maggot-ridden peasants. Plus some nasty collar devices that keep the revolting scum in order. The Covenant need a Groosalugg to do their dirty work for them and couldn't even organise a decent beheading without mucking it up.

Sahjhan

Impressive time-travelling abilities, which mean that Sahjhan can sneakily create false prophecies. But his occasional (and ambiguous) non-corporeality is a definite drawback in any fight to the death. Twitches, rather like a chicken, when his head is cut off, however ('Origin') – which is always good for a laugh.

Daniel Holtz

God-fearing, righteous, mad as *toast*. Holtz's devotion to the cause of fighting evil is highlighted by his killing of his own daughter to prevent her from becoming a vampire ('Quickening'). A more complex and multidimensional character than he may appear, Holtz was always flawed by the one element in his psyche that transparently couldn't change – his ceaseless search for revenge on Angelus and Darla.

In his slightly sinister and sadistic relationship with Justine Cooper (proto-Slayer, quasi-submissive masochist, a woman incapable of dealing with any emotion other than pain), we see glimpses of Holtz's ability to get the most out of those around him. But, the more one hears about how he brought up Connor in Quor-Toth, the more repulsed one is by this bitter, dangerous man. So, definitely in with a chance of winning.

The Beast

Back in the 1780s, the Svear Priestesses' name for The Beast was 'Big Hard Thing', which seems to sum it all up really. The Beast's only real handicap is that his brain, like the rest of him, is made out of rock. If it's a question of standing still while people throw everything they've got at him and hardly flinching (see 'Apocalypse Nowish') then The Beast's your man. If, on the other hand, any *thinking* is involved (see 'Salvage'), forget it.

Jasmine
The human-eating Power That Was has godlike powers and an ability to inflict her will with such persuasion that entire worlds bow down before her. Looking good so far.

There are two fatal flaws that render Jasmine, ultimately, a completely rubbish would-be dominator of worlds, however. Touching her blood reveals her true visage and saying her true name shatters all of the mind-games that she can create ('Peace Out').

Marcus Hamilton
Suave, a sharp-dressed man and a stevedore in bed (just ask Harmony), Marcus was, he notes, fashioned from the essence of The Senior Partners and his blood is filled with their power. Which, ultimately, proves to be his biggest weakness when fighting a vampire ('Not Fade Away').

The Circle of the Black Thorn
A right bunch of journeyman (and woman) evil entities that all get taken out in the space of one night by somewhat obvious frontal attacks and, in one case, a curious case of slave-blood spiking. No match for the Fang Gang and, therefore, a bit crap in a big fight, frankly.

DEUS EX MACHINA

Magical MacGuffins that appear in *Angel* without pre-warning

The film director Alfred Hitchcock once told a story about a man who was sitting on a train opposite someone who had a small cage in which was some obviously ferocious animal. 'What's in the cage?' the man asked. 'A MacGuffin,' came the reply. 'It's to catch the lions on the Scottish moors.' The man thought about this for a moment. 'But there are *no* lions on the Scottish moors,' he noted. 'In that case,' his new acquaintance replied, 'that is *no* MacGuffin.'

Deus ex machina (literal Latin translation: 'a God out of a machine') means any wholly unlikely device in drama which serves the sole purpose of moving the plot along to provide resolution. A MacGuffin, in other words. Like most dramas, *Angel* features its fair share of these.

 The Gem of Amarra
The vampire's equivalent of the Holy Grail, this ring renders any vampire wearing it immune to death. Questing vampires roamed the Earth seeking it for centuries but it was Spike who finally located it, hidden in a crypt under Sunnydale, only to lose it again in a daylight skirmish with

Buffy who, realising the value of the find, sent it to Angel in LA.

Spike followed, determined to regain his prize, and hired persuasive help in the form of an expert vampire torturer, Marcus.

Oz, Cordelia and Doyle rescue Angel but realise that Marcus has double-crossed Spike and, having stolen the ring, is heading for a beach full of children.

A wounded Angel braves the sunlight to fight Marcus and retrieve the ring; then, having enjoyed one perfect sunset, he destroys it, preferring to retain his nocturnal nature and help those who are lost in the darkness of LA ('In the Dark').

The Scroll of Aberjian/ the Shanshu prophecy

Two MacGuffins for the price of one. A collection of ancient prophecies written over four centuries in a dozen different languages, the Scroll of Aberjian is opportunistically stolen by Angel from the vaults of Wolfram & Hart ('Blind Date').

As Wesley struggles to translate the prophecies, he discovers that Angel – the vampire with a soul – is mentioned in connection with the word Shanshu, which Wesley initially translates as 'to die'. To his consternation, Angel readily accepts his seemingly inevitable fate.

The scrolls are vital to Wolfram & Hart's nefarious schemes and, aided by the demon Vocah, they are determined to retrieve them.

Vocah unleashes chaos, murdering the Oracles, inflicting the gift of continuous visions on Cordelia and, having retrieved the scrolls, blowing up Angel's apartment and seriously injuring Wesley.

Angel learns that he can save Cordelia by seeking Vocah at the Raising and finding the words of Anatole within the scrolls. He tracks the Wolfram & Hart team to a mausoleum and interrupts the Raising (a ceremony involving a large crate, several monks and a lot of Latin chanting).

Despite Vocah's death, Lindsey is able to successfully complete the ritual. For his trouble, Angel slices off Lindsey's hand, regains the Scrolls and takes them to the hospital where a convalescent Wesley uses the words of Anatole to restore Cordelia ('To Shanshu in LA').

Wesley later discovers an error in his translation: 'Shanshu' doesn't mean to die but, rather, to live until he dies. Thus, the vampire with a soul, having fulfilled his destiny, will, it seems, become human.

However, celebrations may be premature as Lilah, Holland and the injured Lindsey gather round the crate, which now contains the returned and very much human Darla.

The Shroud of Rahmon

A mystical cloth, dyed in the blood of seven virgins sacrificed on a full moon and placed over the body of the demon Rahmon, thus preventing his resurrection. All who come into contact with the shroud seemingly go mad. Angel and Gunn become involved in a somewhat convoluted plan to steal the shroud ('The Shroud of Rahmon').

The Loa

A powerful entity that can foretell the future. Wesley, perturbed by a prophecy that suggests that Angel will kill his infant son Connor, seeks guidance from the Loa and has his worst fears confirmed: the prophecy's fulfilment will be foreshadowed by earthquake, fire and blood. Moreover, Wesley, himself, is facing a future filled with anguish and betrayal.

The gravity of the warning is, perhaps, undermined by the fact that the Loa's manifestation is in the form of a giant talking hamburger. And a cranky one at that ('Couplet').

The Axis of Pythia

Seeking the whereabouts of the missing Cordelia, Angel visits Dinza, dark goddess of the lost, who tells him of a mystical antiquity, the Axis of Pythia. This can locate souls trapped in other dimensions.

Forged from the tripod of the Delphic Oracle, the Axis is reputed to be worth $33 million, and Angel has a rival in seeking the Axis – glamorous high-voltage cat burglar, Gwen Raiden.

Gwen successfully steals the mystical antiquity, but agrees to loan it to Angel, who uses it to discover that Cordelia is, seemingly, happy in a higher dimension ('Ground State').

The Totems of the Ra-Tet

As The Beast rampages through Los Angeles, the Angel Investigations team discover that it is systematically exterminating all five members of the Ra-Tet, an ancient mystical order associated with the Egyptian sun-god Ra.

The Ra-Tet consists of five Totems: Mesektet, Ashet, Semkhet, Ma'at and Manjet. Once The Beast has all five, he can assemble them and perform a ritual that will, literally, blot out the sun.

Angel and his friends, aided by Gwen, try to protect Manjet, the last Totem, but he is brutally murdered, despite his apparently safe location in the panic room at Gwen's home.

Despite their best efforts, the team are unable to stop The Beast from joining the Totems and, as he completes the ritual, LA is plunged into perpetual darkness and chaos.

 Magical memory wipe
As the Angel Investigations team are given personalised tours of Wolfram & Hart, Connor – traumatised by his experiences with Jasmine – has become dangerously unstable. Angel is shown the full extent of Connor's torment and is forced to fulfil the prophecy and 'kill' his own son.

However, Lilah Morgan, attempting to persuade Angel to accept The Senior Partner's offer of taking over Wolfram & Hart's LA branch, has apparently made a deal. The team are startled to find that Angel has made an executive decision and signed the contracts on their behalf.

Moreover, none of them have any knowledge of anyone called Connor. History and memories have been magically altered and Connor is now living his life as a normal teenager. Only Angel himself remembers that he ever had a son ('Home'). However, Connor retains his superstrength and, when his troubled parents bring him to Wolfram &

Hart, Angel is forced to confront the consequences of his actions.

Angel trains his son to fulfil another ancient prophecy and kill the demon Sahjhan. But Wesley, having been alerted to the fact that Fred's memories were altered, finds a way to reverse the mind-wipe and restore his own shattered memories. Then he really wishes he hadn't ('Origin').

That mysterious amulet
Offered to Angel as part of the package deal designed to persuade him to accept the gift of Wolfram & Hart, the amulet is designed to play a major role in the coming apocalyptic battle in Sunnydale and comes with a useful file of instructions ('Home').

Despite the amulet's not even remotely reliable source, Angel stills takes it to Sunnydale to help Buffy in her fight against The First Evil. As the amulet is designed to be worn by someone ensouled but more than human, Angel assumes that he will be the chosen champion.

He is, therefore, less than impressed when Buffy sends him back to LA to prepare a second front. And he's positively petulant when he realises that he has a rival in the form of a newly ensouled Spike.

Spike is chosen by Buffy to bear the amulet in battle and he selflessly dies in a pillar of fire as his fabulous accessory blasts out rays of pure sunlight to destroy the army of Übervampires.

But the essence of Spike is retained within the amulet and, when the artefact is mysteriously mailed back to Angel's new office at Wolfram & Hart, it disgorges a furious and incorporeal Spike ('Conviction').

The big box
Spike has something of a problem. Having been toasted and ghosted, his incorporeal nature is making his life difficult. Despite Fred's best efforts, a solution seems no nearer to hand. However, salvation comes in the form of a parcel, mysteriously delivered to Wolfram & Hart's reception desk. (With all of these mysterious packages arriving, causing mayhem and shenanigans, wouldn't you have thought they'd simply stop opening the mail?)

An obliging Harmony opens the box and, after a brief flash and whoosh, Spike attempts to leave, only to walk straight into a door. Spike has his body back and Harmony is once again called upon to oblige with a little celebratory road test.

But Spike's recorporealisation has potentially catastrophic side-effects as the presence of two ensouled vampires apparently throws the universe into chaos ('Destiny').

The Cup Of Perpetual Torment
According to the Shanshu Prophecy, the vampire with a soul – a true champion – will play a pivotal role in the apocalypse.

But *which* vampire with a soul? It had always been assumed (chiefly by Angel himself) that the prophecy referred to Angel. However, since Spike's unselfish sacrifice saved the world, there are now two candidates. And, according to Eve, the wheel of destiny is spinning off its axis, causing a wave of madness to sweep through Wolfram & Hart.

In the absence of Wesley, Angel seeks help from a member of his department, the erudite ex-Watcher Douglas Sirk.

Sirk reads some newly translated verses from the prophecy. The vampire with a soul must drink from the Cup of Perpetual Torment. He will *then* have the weight of the worlds upon him, binding his limbs and grinding his bones to meal until he saves creation or destroys it. At which point he will have his past wiped clean and will become human.

After a chequered history, the cup in question is now conveniently located in Death Valley at The Columns, an opera house buried in the 1930s by an earthquake. Angel and Spike race to Nevada, each determined to prove that he is the predestined champion.

Spike is disappointed by his first sight of the cup. He rather thought it would be a little less goldeny, what with all the torment and everything. But, after a knock-down drag-out brawl with Angel, he stands victorious and, despite Angel's warnings of the consequences of what he is about to do, he drinks from the cup.

Which, it turns out, contains not perpetual torment but rather Mountain Dew. The pair have been duped ('Destiny').

'SUBTEXT RAPIDLY BECOMING THE TEXT'

20 exterior sources that provided inspiration to, or are referenced in, *Angel*

Like many modern TV series (*24*, *Stargate SG-1*, *The Simpsons* and *The X-Files* are contemporary examples), *Angel* appears to be the product of our increasingly interconnected multimedia age. In other words, it's a show produced by a bunch of thirtysomething fanboy (and fangirl) media-geeks who revel in knowingly sampling exterior texts into their work.

They do this openly, in the belief that their audience are sussed enough to know what they're watching a homage to and, thus, to join in a celebration of that twilight *demi-monde* world somewhere between parody and tribute.

Intellectual parallelograms crop up all over the place in *Angel*, in an outrageous mix of pop-culture allusions, acknowledged roots, visual references and aspects that may owe a more subtle debt to other texts. There has never, at any stage, been a suggestion of intentional plagiarism, it should be noted. Rather, *Angel*'s writers and directors have, whether consciously or unconsciously, defined their audience as a collective who have, more or less, the same DVD and comics collections that they, themselves, do.

Thus, in *Angel*, we're treated to a never-ending stream of references: pop-culture, 'Generation X' and general homage to all things esoteric. This section contains a sampling.

Apart from the very Gotham City-look of twilight Los Angeles and Angel walking down the alley at the end of both the tag-sequence of 'City Of' and the subsequent title sequence with his coat billowing behind him like a cape, the pilot episode also saw the first of many direct *Batman* references within the show, Doyle noting that Angel's home has a Bat-cave feel to it. Allusions to the Caped Crusader, his slightly gay chum Robin, and his rogues gallery of psychopathic nemeses also occur in 'Lonely Heart', 'In the Dark', 'Rm W/a Vu', 'Expecting', 'She', 'Waiting in the Wings', 'Benediction', 'Ground State', 'Release', 'Inside Out', 'Smile Time', 'Underneath' and 'Time Bomb'.

Doyle being half-human on his mother's side is a characteristic he shares not only with Mr Spock in *Star Trek* and the Doctor in *Doctor Who*, but also with Jesus, the mythical Hercules of *Legendary Journeys* and many other literary and comic-book characters.

The 'Johnny Depp once-over', mentioned during 'In the Dark', refers to the hotel-wrecking antics of the authors' favourite actor, celebrity *Fast Show*-fan and occasional Oasis slide-guitarist, the star of *21 Jump Street*, *Cry-Baby*, *Edward Scissorhands*, *Ed Wood*, *Donnie Brasco*, *Sleepy Hollow* and *From Hell*. Depp is also mentioned in 'Just Rewards' along with his *Pirates of the Caribbean* co-star Orlando Bloom.

Aspects of one of the most infamous murder trials of the twentieth century, OJ Simpson's acquittal of killing his wife in 1995, are alluded to in several episodes along with some

235

of the case's key players such as Simpson's controversial lawyer Johnny Cochran and Mark Fuhrman, the detective who was accused of racism as a major plank of the defence's case. References occur in 'I Fall to Pieces', 'Sense and Sensitivity', 'Conviction' and 'The Cautionary Tale of Numero Cinco'.

Wesley's middle name is a probable tribute to the king of British science fiction, John Wyndham (1903–1969), the author of *The Day of the Triffids*, *The Midwich Cuckoos*, *The Kraken Wakes* and *Random Quest*.

In 'She', Angel describes the painting *La Music Aux Tuileries* by French Impressionist Edouard Manet (1832–83) to an enthralled gallery audience: he notes that in the middle distance is the artist's friend, the poet Charles Baudelaire (1821–1867). Angel quotes from the latter's poem, *Le Vampyr*, and suggests that speculation exists that the poem was about a *real* vampire. And, also, that Baudelaire was actually a little taller and a lot drunker than depicted in the painting.

During 'Eternity', Rebecca talks about her idea of vampires being Bela Lugosi and Gary Oldman. Angel replies that Frank Langella's was the only cinematic performance he ever believed. This refers to the actors who played the Count in *Dracula* (1931), *Bram Stoker's Dracula* (1992) and *Dracula* (1979) respectively. No Christopher Lee? Philistines.

The title of 'Are You Now or Have You Ever Been?' was a phrase made infamous during the House UnAmerican Committee hearings of 1947 and 1951. HUAC, and notably senator Joseph McCarthy, interrogated Americans about alleged leftist connections, holding witnesses in contempt if they refused to answer. The investigation of various Hollywood radicals by HUAC turned into a media circus when some of the first witnesses refused to co-operate. Congress cited 10 witnesses (including noted film director Edward Dmytryk) for contempt and by mid-1950 most had served one-year prison terms.

During an online interview, Tim Minear, the author of 'Are You Now or Have You Ever Been?' listed various movies that he had alluded to in the script, some obvious, others oblique. These included: *Barton Fink*, *Rebel Without a Cause*, *Chinatown*, *Vertigo*, *LA Confidential*, *Psycho* and *The Hudsucker Proxy*. Angel's room in the Hyperion, 217, is a reference to Stephen King's *The Shining*.

The titular artefact in 'The Shroud of Rahmon' is – fairly obviously – influenced by the Shroud of Turin which, for centuries, was purported to be the burial garment of Christ. Preserved, since 1578, in the Cathedral of San Giovanni Battista in Turin, it features two faint images of a man and contains markings that roughly correspond to the stigmata wounds of Jesus as described in the gospels. First historically recorded when put on display by Templar Knight Geoffroi de Charnay in 1389, it was contemporaneously denounced as fake by the Bishop of Troyes. In 1988 the age of the cloth was determined by carbon dating as between 1260 and 1390.

In 'Carpe Noctem', Fred believes that Angel's reading list may include Fyodor Dostoyevski's *The Brothers Karamazov* and the work of James Joyce (1882–1941:

237

Ulysses, Finnegans Wake) and Johann Wolfgang von Goethe (1749–1832: *Faust, Iphigenie auf Tauris*). She also suggests that Angel's inability to experience love is worthy of F Scott Fitzgerald (1896–1940: *Tender is the Night, The Great Gatsby, The Last Tycoon*).

'The road to Hell is paved with good intentions,' quoted in 'Loyalty', was first attributed to St Bernard of Clairvaux (1090–1153) by St Francis of Sales (1567–1622). Variations of the phrase have been used by, among others, George Herbert in *Jacula Pruentum*, John Ray in *English Proverbs*, Samuel Johnson and George Bernard Shaw in *Maxims for Revolutionists*.

Lilah asks in 'Tomorrow' if Connor isn't something without precedent in human history. Wesley notes that, on the contrary, Greek, Mesopotamian, Hindi and Celtic myth, the Bible, and even Charles Darwin's theory of evolution, all support the coming of something that wasn't previously possible.

Lorne's narration in 'Spin the Bottle' (and breaking the fourth wall when commenting on various characters' stupidity) was possibly inspired by similar techniques used in Thornton Wilder's *Our Town* – although addressing the audience directly from inside a play is a trick that even Shakespeare used (cf. *Macbeth*'s ten-line soliloquy, *Hamlet*'s musings on life and death, etc.). One of Wesley's theories about what's happening is that all of those trapped in the Hyperion with amnesia are strangers brought together by a mysterious evil who is, in fact, one of them – the basic premise of Agatha Christie's *And Then There Were None*.

'Awakening' includes references to 'the nine Antediluvian Patriarchs' in Genesis (the biblical line of Noah's ancestors that includes Adam, Seth, Enos, Cainan, Mehalaleel, Jared, Enoch, Methuselah and Lamech). There's also a reference to Rashi – one of the most important Jewish sages of the Middle Ages. His commentaries on the Bible and the Talmud are still regarded as essential to fully understanding the texts.

Visually and conceptually Wesley's confrontation with the caged Angelus in 'Soulless' comes from *The Silence of the Lambs* and the dazzling mind-games played by Hannibal Lecter on his *alleged* interrogator, Clarice Starling.

In 'Shiny Happy People', Jasmine notes that The Powers That Be merely observe humanity and refuse to interfere, similar to the attitude of the Time Lords in *Doctor Who* and The Elders in *Charmed*. The episode also includes allusions to the concept of ego-death via Carl Jung's conceptual 'oceanic consciousness', Aldous Huxley's visions of Zen utopianism and Timothy Leary and Richard Alpert's *The Psychedelic Experience* ('we are all one'). What a load of tree-hugging hippy *crap*.

Fred visits a bookstore looking for literature on mass hypnosis. The owner believes that he has implants in his head that allow the CIA access to his thoughts. (There's a reference to MK-ULTRA, the CIA's notorious programme of mind control.) The store is named The Magic Bullet, which takes viewers to a whole sub-genre of conspiracy theory via *JFK*, *The X-Files* and its spin-off *The Lone Gunmen*.

Jasmine subsequently rewards the owner's loyalty by assuring him, in all sincerity, that in Dallas, on 22 November 1963, Lee Oswald acted alone. With a manual bolt-action Mannlicher-Carcano rifle. Hitting a moving target at 90 yards, through dense foliage. In exactly 5.6 seconds (as established by Abraham Zapruder's film). Well, *that* sounds reasonable.

In 'Hellbound', Spike notes that he and Angel seem to be stuck together in some kind of permanent double act, like Bob Hope and Bing Crosby. From the mention of Crosby, his train of thought wanders to a litany that includes Stephen Stills and Graham Nash (formerly of Buffalo Springfield and the Hollies respectively and, together with David Crosby and Neil Young, members of CSNY) and then, bizarrely, on to the 70s buddy-sitcom *Chico and the Man* (starring the late Freddie Prinze).

'My hat's off to the movie *U-571* and *Submarines for Dummies* which were my main resources,' noted Steven DeKnight shortly after 'Why We Fight' aired. The title comes from a series of information films made by Frank Capra for the US War Department during the period 1942–45. Conceptually, the episode is a mixture of *Das Boot*, *Miracleman* and those flashback episodes – like 'Apocrypha' and 'Triangle' – that *The X-Files* used to do so successfully. Sam Lawson was the name of a character (played by Cliff Robertson) in Robert Aldrich's Second World War drama *Too Late the Hero*.

'Not Fade Away' was a 1958 hit for Buddy Holly and the Crickets and was subsequently covered by numerous acts including – most famously – the Rolling Stones. (It was also, as several media commentators noted when the episode was broadcast, often performed live by one of David Boreanaz's favourite bands, the Grateful Dead.) There's also a possible allusion to lyrics by Joss Whedon's beloved Neil Young in 'My My Hey Hey'. Conceptually, some of the episode's inspiration appears to have come from two influential DC comic series, *The Sandman* (the conceit of a, literal, hope in Hell) and *Hellblazer*.

'ZAP! BAM! POW!'

Comic book characters referenced or alluded to in *Angel*

- The Fantastic Four ('In the Dark', 'Slouching Towards Bethlehem').

- Casper the Friendly Ghost ('Rm W/a Vu', 'Apocalypse Nowish', 'Just Rewards').

- Captain America ('The Ring', 'Why We Fight').

- Superman ('Blind Date', 'Ground State', 'Apocalypse Nowish', 'Destiny', 'Soul Purpose').

- Gunn's anti-racist speech to Wolfram & Hart in 'Blind Date' appears to be influenced by similar sentiments expressed in an issue of the late-60s *Green Lantern/Green Arrow*.

- Neil Gaiman's The Sandman ('The Price').

- Vampirella ('Deep Down').

- Electro Girl ('Ground State').

- The Ghost ('Supersymmetry').

- Dardevil ('Supersymmetry').

- The Hulk ('Supersymmetry').

- Supergirl ('Release').

- The Prez ('Players').
- The Legion of Doom ('Inside Out').
- Spider-Man ('Inside Out', 'Smile Time').
- The Punisher ('Conviction').
- The Uncanny X-Men ('Conviction').
- The Tick ('Just Rewards').
- The Flash ('Shells').
- Swamp Thing ('The Girl in Question').

LOGIC, LET ME INTRODUCE YOU TO THIS WINDOW (PART 2)

Even more things in *Angel* that make absolutely no logical sense whatsoever

 In 'To Shanshu in LA', watch the doughnut that Wesley and Cordelia share. It's never in the same half-eaten condition two shots running.

 Angel says that 'caritas' is Latin for mercy in 'Judgment'. It isn't, it's Greek for charity.

 There are numerous anachronisms in 'Are You Now or Have You Ever Been?' When the money stolen in 1952 is seen, it's in new $100 bills – with the 'big' Ben Franklin head – which weren't minted until the 1990s. In the Hollywood Blvd bookstore a star from the Walk of Fame can be seen. The first star wasn't placed on the street until February 1960.

There's also a 1970s-style telephone on the wall along with a poster for a Flying Circus that appears to be photocopied (something not possible in 1952). The TV in the hotel lobby is not a 1950s model. Certainly the screen (it looks about 18 inches) is way too big.

Anybody else notice the same three vintage cars driving up and down outside the Hyperion in the 1952 sequences? In the blending shot from the present day photo of the Hyperion to 1952, although the hotel seems to go from run down to good condition, the trees and bushes around it are all exactly the same.

In *Buffy*: 'Angel', Angel swore that after 1898 and the gypsy girl, he had never killed another human being. 'Darla', 'Orpheus' and 'Why We Fight' all suggest otherwise.

If the Groosalugg can *only* mate with a human and, according to the prophecy, is destined to mate with the princess, then why are the Covenant so surprised that their monarch is human ('Through the Looking Glass')? From the same episode, Numfar's Dance of Joy and Dance of Honour seem to be, more or less, the same – though maybe that's the whole point.

In the 1764 sequences in 'Quickening', nobody in York has any semblance of an English accent, much less a Yorkshire one.

Considering that the final scenes of 'Lullaby' are taking place in what seems like a monsoon, there are several close-up shots in which Julie Benz and David Boreanaz don't seem to be getting rained on at all.

In the same episode Lilah tells Gavin that Wolfram & Hart don't crucify their enemies as 'It's too Christian'. While it is an important part of Christian iconography, the actual practice of crucifixion wasn't Christian *at all*; it was a

Roman method of execution used *on* Christians. And anybody else they didn't like, of various faiths.

There's a clear suggestion that Angel gets an erection when he and Cordelia are investigating backstage at the ballet in 'Waiting in the Wings'. How is this possible for a vampire whose heart doesn't beat?

At what point does Jasmine take control of Cordelia's actions? 'Inside Out' suggests it's from the moment that Lorne gave her the reversal spell in 'Spin the Bottle' and, certainly, the authors are sure many fans will agree with us that we'd all like to think she was *possessed* when she slept with Connor. However, her actions in 'Habeas Corpses' and several subsequent episodes simply don't support this.

Pacoima is said to be about 25 minutes drive from the Hyperion ('Soulless'). By *helicopter*, possibly. More like an hour even if the traffic is relatively light. *Angel*'s Los Angeles is clearly the same one seen in *24*, where people can get from one side of the metropolis to the other in just minutes.

For Fred's plan to work in 'The Magic Bullet', Angel needed to be standing directly behind Jasmine when Fred fired the gun. A few inches to either side and the bullet simply wouldn't have hit Angel and, thus, cured him. Afterwards, the bullet looks remarkably intact after going through Jasmine's dense skin and tough bone, before emerging and hitting Angel. Where have we heard *that* before?

The timeline for almost all of Season 4 is *really* confusing. On the face of it, the entire season seems to take place over the course of about six weeks. However, individual episodes include frequently contradictory references to the passage of time since some previous event.

For instance, in 'Players' it's suggested that it has been several weeks since the unleashing of Angelus, completely contradicting implications given during the previous four episodes that they all took place over about two days.

In 'Sacrifice', Golden says that his group have been hiding in the sewers for two weeks. When they went down, the sun was still blocked, placing those events pre-'Salvage'. Which means that everything from then onwards has taken place in a fortnight, making further nonsense of the dating of Cordelia's pregnancy.

One knows that LA is a city of some strange sights but doesn't *anyone* notice the wholly conspicuous green man (wearing shades and a hat just to make him stand out a bit more) sitting in the courtroom of a major criminal trial ('Conviction')? From this moment on it seems as though the production team just gave up on the concept of Lorne's appearance being, in any way, unusual.

Another timescale query: in 'Home', Angel is offered the opportunity to run Wolfram & Hart by Lilah; she also gives him the amulet which, after a short stop to make sure Connor's new life is going OK, Angel subsequently gives to Buffy. (One would presume this happened on the same day – it's only an 80-mile drive from LA to Sunnydale.)

The next day, Buffy and her friends fought The First Evil's forces and Spike closed the Hellmouth. Back in LA, it's reasonable to assume that Angel and co. spent a couple of days tying up their affairs at the Hyperion and moving into Wolfram & Hart (indeed, in 'Conviction', Fred is seen carrying a box of her things into the firm as though it's her first day).

It is, however, established during that episode that Angel and co. have been at Wolfram & Hart for 'a few days' (perhaps as much as a week). The events of 'Conviction' take place over the course of one day and, at the end of it, Spike arrives. At the beginning of 'Just Rewards', we're informed that the events of *Buffy*: 'Chosen' happened 19 days ago when, in the timeline established, it should have been no more than eight or nine (see 'Unleashed' for some further complications).

When Angel talks about attending the first episode of *The Carol Burnett Show* ('Not Fade Away') he mentions that Tim Conway was on fire that night. Although comedian Conway *was* a regular on the show, he was not featured in the first episode (when Carol's guest was singer Jim Nabors). Conway's first appearance was actually in episode four.

'LET'S GO TO WORK'

12 classic lines of dialogue from *Angel*'s Season 5

- Angel's speed-dialer: 'You have reached Ritual Sacrifice. For Goats, press one or say "Goats".' ('Conviction')

- Spike: 'I must be in Hell.' Lorne: 'No, LA, but a lot of people make that mistake.' ('Just Rewards')

- Angel: 'Eve, you stay here with me and we'll have more sex.' ('Life of the Party')

- Harmony, to Fred: 'I wish I were more like you. Except for the part about being all into science. And not having a lot up-front.' ('Harm's Way')

- Angel on Spike: 'He's ... is "pathological idiot" an actual condition?' ('Damage')

- Angel: 'With these resources, there's no one we can't save.' Cordelia: 'Except, maybe, yourself.' ('You're Welcome')

- Puppet-Angel, to Nina: 'I'm made of felt. And my nose comes off.' ('Smile Time')

- Spike: 'I figure, there's a bloke, somewhere around New Zealand, standing on a bridge like this, looking back at us. There's a hole in the world ... We ought to've known.' ('A Hole in the World')

- Illyria: 'Your breed is fragile. How is it they came to control this world?' Knox: 'Opposable thumbs. Fire. Television.' ('Shells')

- Illyria: 'When the world met me, it shuddered. Groaned. It knelt at my feet.' Spike: 'Dear *Penthouse*, I don't normally write letters like this, but ...' ('Time Bomb')

- Alfonso: 'Look, the Americans are relying on violence to solve the problem. What a surprise.' ('The Girl in Question')

- Lindsey, on The Circle: 'It's a secret society.' Gunn: 'Never heard of them.' Lindsey: 'That's cos they're *secret*.' ('Power Play')

DEATH OR GLORY

Five season-ending cliffhangers that shaped the future of
Angel

 Angel and Wesley are staying with Cordelia in the aftermath of the destruction of their office and the horrors that Cordy and Wes have recently been through: Cordelia notes that they have lots of evil to fight and lots of people to help, something that her horrifying visions have impressed upon her.

Suddenly, Wesley realises that he had incorrectly translated the word Shanshu found in the ancient prophecy. It appears to suggest that far from predicting Angel's death, the prophecy is stating that, one day, he will become human.

Meanwhile, at Wolfram & Hart, Lilah, Holland and Lindsey enter the vault where the box from the ritual is being stored. Lilah looks into the box and tells whatever is inside that she knows it's a bit confusing but that it will soon get better. Inside the box is ... Darla ('To Shanshu in LA').

 Angel, Cordelia, Wesley, Gunn, Lorne and Fred have returned from their adventures in Pylea via a portal that lands Angel's car back in the middle of Caritas. Lorne asks if they want a nightcap.

Returning to the Hyperion, Angel enters the hotel saying, 'There's no place like ...' only to find a sad-looking Willow sitting in the lobby waiting to inform him of Buffy's death ('There's No Place Like Plrtz Glrb').

With Cordelia having ascended to a higher plane of existence, Angel finds himself victim of a trap set by his own son. Connor and Justine lower the lid of Angel's coffin into place and then weld it shut. They push the coffin off the boat and watch as it sinks to the bottom of the ocean.

At the Hyperion, Gunn and Fred find themselves alone. Fred wonders where everybody went ('Tomorrow').

The Angel Investigations team have been offered the opportunity of a lifetime: to take over Wolfram & Hart's LA branch. Most, for their own reasons, think it's an offer worth accepting. Angel, however, has accepted anyway, having cut a deal with Lilah and The Senior Partners.

It's getting dark as Angel watches through the window of a family home. There, he sees Connor, safely given a new life with a new family, celebrating his graduation from high school and looking forward to college. Satisfied, if a little sad, Angel gets into his waiting limo and is driven away ('Home').

In the alley behind the Hyperion, having learned of Wesley's heroic sacrifice, Angel, Spike, Illyria and a badly injured Gunn face the vast armies of Hell, including a dragon. Gunn suggests that the others should take the 30,000 on the left. Illyria tells him that he will last 10 minutes at best, but Gunn believes that he can make those minutes count.

Spike asks what the plan is. We fight, replies Angel. Then he adds, 'Personally, I wanna slay the dragon. Let's go to work!' ('Not Fade Away').

DID YOU KNOW ...?

20 bits of completely useless trivia that defy categorisation

 When it comes to the stunts on *Angel*, David Boreanaz told *The Big Breakfast*: 'I do as many as I possibly can. Of course the producers don't want me to ... My stuntperson, Mike Massa, does [about] 80 per cent.'

 The Angel Investigations building used in Season 1 was located on a soundstage at Paramount Studios on Melrose Avenue, not far from the *Star Trek: Voyager* bridge. Both sets were close to the CrashDown Café from *Roswell*. Paramount, where most of Angel's interior scenes were shot, was also where sitcoms like *Happy Days* and *Mork & Mindy* were filmed. One of the portals to Pylea (seen in 'Over the Rainbow') was the entrance to Paramount.

 During Charisma Carpenter's time as a cheerleader in San Diego she and two male friends were at the beach one night when they were confronted by an armed man. He ordered Charisma to tie up her friends with the clear intention that he'd then rape her.

With astonishing bravery and a gun held to her head, Charisma refused and, in the ensuing commotion, the

group were able to fight off the man who fled, shooting and wounding one of Charisma's friends. Their witness statements eventually led to the arrest of the assailant, a police officer and serial rapist. A dramatisation of the incident was filmed by the Discovery Channel's *The Justice Files*, featuring an interview with Charisma herself.

Many of the drawings on the *Demons, Demons, Demons* database are sketches by Joss Whedon, used to create the monsters for *Buffy* and *Angel*. These include the Kailiff from 'Rm W/a Vu', a Kawaini from 'The Prodigal' and a Brachen demon from 'Hero'.

It was reported in July 2001 that David Boreanaz had purchased a home in Sunset Strip. Built in 1936, the house was a Cape Cod-style, 1,700 square feet with two bedrooms and a pool. The asking price was just under $1.3 million.

Alexis Denisof's hobbies include scuba diving, horse riding and skiing. 'I skied all my life,' he told an Internet interview. 'I had a much more adventurous childhood than Wesley did. I moved around a lot, going between the Pacific Northwest and New England. And I lived in England when I was a teenager.' Asked what he missed most about England, Alexis replied: 'The newspapers, the tea, the sense of a city centre, which LA lacks. I miss the culture of theatre, art galleries, music, and every conceivable art form.'

In 2000, it was widely reported that David Boreanaz was suing the driver of a car that crashed into his on 3 August 1999. According to the Los Angeles Superior Court lawsuit, Oren Kaniel's Mazda ran into the actor's Mercedes-

Benz on the Ventura Freeway. Boreanaz alleged that he was 'hurt and injured in his health, strength, and activity', and suffered 'injury to [his] nervous system'.

The highlight of the Nocturnal 3K convention at the Radisson Hotel in Heathrow was Andy Hallett's perform-ance of 'Lady Marmalade' and 'Superstition' (the latter in a duet with J August Richards) while Joss Whedon found himself 'surrounded by a blanket of starry-eyed girlies,' according to *SFX*. As James Marsters pogo'd to an assem-bled throng of 'swooning hearts and damp panties', Andy Hallett was heard to declare: 'This place is a *bomb*. We wanna live here!'

J August Richards attended the University of Southern California with *Buffy* actors Danny Strong and George Hertzberg.

'Billy' was a work-in-progress *Angel* script on 11 September 2001. Tim Minear recalls that he was writing the script when a friend called and told him to turn on his TV to watch events unfolding in New York. Two of the episode's most impressive scenes – Angel and, subse-quently, Cordelia visiting Lilah's apartment – were written by Joss Whedon specifically so that Minear could attend a reading at Whedon's house.

On Channel 4's *T4* interview with David Boreanaz in January 2002, there was confirmation of a dreadful rumour that had been doing the rounds. Yes David is, indeed, a Manchester United supporter. Well, *that*'s unsurprising. He only lives 5,000 miles away from Old Trafford, which makes him a local boy compared to many of their fans.

On 24 March 2003, at Cedar Sinai hospital in Beverly Hills, Charisma Carpenter gave birth to her and partner Damien Hardy's first child, a boy named Donavan.

 Although professing himself not to be a particularly rabid fan of Barry Manilow, the first concert that the teenage David Boreanaz attended in Philadelphia was, he admitted to Rob Francis, one featuring the gargantuan-nosed 'Mandy' singer/songwriter.

 'I asked David Boreanaz from *Angel* to be in it,' noted British singer Dido Armstrong concerning David's appearance in the video for her single 'White Flag'. 'I wanted someone dark and young. He's a lot of fun and was really up for it even though it was something he didn't have to do.'

 Alexis Denisof's absence from 'Destiny' was due to him being on his honeymoon with his wife Alyson Hannigan.

Shortly before shooting for Season 5 began, Alexis developed a condition known as Bell's Palsy, which partially paralysed one side of his face temporarily. He still hadn't fully recovered when 'Conviction' was recorded so, in almost every scene, he was filmed in profile.

 James Marsters fronted his own Clash and Nirvana-influenced band, Ghost of the Robot, as an outlet for his musical passion. Along with bandmates Aaron Anderson, Steven Sellars, Kevin McPherson and Charlie DeMars, James toured with the band extensively during 2003/04 when his *Buffy* and *Angel* filming duties allowed.

257

Via the Internet, the band released three singles – 'David Letterman', 'Valerie' and 'A New Man' – the album *Mad Brilliant* (which, purely coincidentally, included a song called 'Angel') and an EP, *It's Nothing*. The full set goes for around £150 on e-Bay. They split before they could release their final CD, *Gods of the Radio*, though several of the songs from its sessions were aired live during their 2004 European tour, including the saucy 'Bad', a tale of a one-night-stand at a convention.

In 2005 James launched his debut solo CD *Civilized Man*, with a sold-out tour of the UK (including a show at the legendary Cavern Club). An estimated 10,000 people turned out to Collectormania 7 in Milton Keynes, in the hope of getting one of the 2,000 James Marsters autograph tickets on offer. (Anthony Head and Alexis Denisof also did a brisk trade at the same event.)

James apologised for rarely personalising autographs, explaining that anything other than his usual signature causes pain in his hand, which was broken during an altercation in a church basement during his theatre days. The local pastor interrupted rehearsals at a critical moment and an infuriated Marsters punched the stage, which was made of concrete. James still believes that it would probably have been better for all concerned if he'd just punched the preacher instead.

 In the original shooting script for 'Why We Fight', the two men who came to Angel's apartment in 1943 to persuade him to undertake the mission were identified as Commander Petrie and Mr Fury – references to *Buffy* writer Doug Petrie and *Angel* writer/producer David Fury.

However, neither name is mentioned in the episode itself or on the credits.

 One item of *Buffy*-related merchandise released during 2003 allowed Juliet Landau to follow in an established family tradition. 'I have an action figure [based on Drusilla]. My parents have that too,' she gleefully told *Xposé*. 'My sister was saying, "I'm the only one in the family without a doll, it isn't fair!"' Juliet's mum and dad were, of course, TV icons of a previous generation, Barbara Bain and Martin Landau, the stars of *Mission: Impossible* and *Space: 1999*.

 Since *Angel*'s cancellation, David Boreanaz's career has, literally, gone to the dogs. At least, that's the headline *TV Guide* used when reporting, in July 2004, that David had been recruited by the pressure group People for the Ethical Treatment of Animals to appear in a public-service campaign urging dog owners not to chain their pets in the yard.

 The genesis for 'Waiting in the Wings' was a chance remark by Amy Acker that she had studied ballet as a teenager. Intended to showcase Amy's skills, the episode was constructed around a fantasy sequence that featured Fred and Wesley dancing on stage. Though filmed, this scene was cut from the final episode. Thankfully it *was* added as an extra to the *Angel* Season 3 DVD set.

HERE'S WHERE THE STORY ENDS

The bit you probably *don't* want to read …

From the evidence of 'Not Fade Away' we know, or can speculate, the following about what happened to these characters that we've grown to know so well.

- Angel: Dead.

- Wesley: Dead.

- Gunn: Dead.

- Spike: Dead.

- Illyria: Dead.

It's not as satisfying or happy a future for Angel and his friends as it was for the Scooby Gang after the closing of the Hellmouth. But, given the dangerous and vital nature of the work they did, it was probably an inevitable one.[1]

They died as Champions, fighting the good fight not because it was the *easy* thing to do, but because it was the *right* thing to do.

[1] Or alternatively – if you *desperately* need to believe in miracles – Angel, Spike and Illyria slew the dragon, defeated seemingly impossible odds and lived to mourn their fallen comrades and fight another day.

Angel, like it's sister-show, told perhaps uncomfortable stories the way that they had to be told – whether the audience wanted or even *deserved* them or not.

They ultimately reminded us that fighting for what you believe in is important and that, sometimes, the only thing that matters is that you *did* fight.